13
Enlightenment

— A timeless story that brings you to the core of your true nature and the end of suffering

by Vic Shayne

© 2018 by Vic Shayne
Published by
Creative Bureau Enterprises,
Colorado, USA

This book may not be reproduced either in whole or part by any means, including but not limited to electronically, digitally, by scanning, manually, and/or by audio recording without the expressed written consent of the author.

ISBN-13: 978-1724469762
ISBN-10: 1724469762

*In appreciation of
my teachers Ellie Roozdar and Janice Shayne
for helping me know that which has been here all along*

All that I know is that I am.
I can know that the self is not me, because I can inquire into it, deconstruct it until it seems to dissolve, or just leave it alone, and yet I still exist. The body is not me, because it appears, changes, and eventually ceases to exist. Consciousness, too, is heir to movement and impermanence, and I am not solely that either. What remains when all else is removed is the silence that is a still, infinite, boundless, permanent, un-cancellable nothingness from which all springs.
And this Absoluteness never changes.
I can only say that I am this.

My simple story

I am neither a monk nor a holy man, sage nor seer. I am but a simple man who once sought desperately and intently to find the Truth that lies behind the fabric of life itself. Arising from this search for my own true nature I have left a trail of so-named *Pillars* so that the next seeker may use them as a guide to uncover this one and only Truth. Woven into my story are these Pillars. They do not suggest or teach, and they do not provide answers to the great unknown. They are not the words of authority, nor do they serve as a method. They only point the way, acting as a framework or addendum to the unexplainable. There is nothing to be described or transmitted about the ultimate Truth. By earnestly inquiring into your true nature, you may come to realize it; but this must be done by you alone. No one can say "I am" on your behalf.

I ask nothing more of you than to leave every idea, memory, and judgment behind as you read this story. But if you glorify it, read between the lines, bend it to your own image, study it as a map, or judge it against your religious beliefs or philosophy, then you will miss the simplicity of its message. To know yourself at the deepest level will take your full attention, because without your attention there can be no way of taking my story and finding the ultimate Truth, in your own way. If this does not occur, then my words will only remain words, devoid of meaning or help.

Perhaps you'll meet a guru who will lead you to the gate of your own being. That is up to all of the conditions that have created you and brought you to these very pages. All I can do for you is to tell you my story.

Please keep in mind that self-discovery is not about ideas, learning, flashes of light, wisdom, or even seeking. And it is not an exciting experience that you may adequately relate to others. No, it is something so much deeper, because it is uncovering the depths of your Self as consciousness. This takes tremendous attention and courage, because it requires being yourself without the mind that was built upon the past; it ultimately means bringing the belief that is the ego, or small self, or "I," to an end. Until you go deeply into this process you will never realize just how conditioned you have been, so that the freedom you seek is truly only from the ego itself; and there really is nothing to attain. The Truth is always now; how could it be otherwise?

As you read my words, try to keep in mind that, despite great care and intent, language fails to accurately convey what cannot be described. Words turn actuality — the present Absolute of all that is — into a concept, an object. But, since we have nothing more than words, so much may seem paradoxical, confusing, or mystical. But remember this: There is nothing mystical here except to the mind.

My story is not an instructional means of telling you how to achieve enlightenment or self-realization, because this is not how such things come about. Instead, I am relating a series of events and principles — pillars — that led me gradually toward uncovering the Truth of who I am and the very nature of reality. Such pillars are not dictates, images, nor methods, but merely small discoveries I made along the way. In the end, however, all thoughts, memories, principles, ideas, searching, mentation, and methodologies must be abandoned, because these are no more than artifacts of the self.

While there is much ground to cover, I will say that it is most helpful to place your attention on the meaning of the word "I," and what it actually represents.

And now my story…

My search for the ultimate truth

Very little happens where I am from — a rather small and insignificant village where, for most of the year, the sun beats mercilessly on the land, animals, plants, and people, and then, during the monsoon season, the rain comes down in blinding sheets from the sky to fill the rivers, flood the plains, top off the wells, and nourish the fields. The vegetation is lush, and the verdant jungle teems with plants and animals that coexist, live, thrive, fight, struggle, and then die according to the flow and cycles of nature. At the edge of the jungle are sunbaked beaches of endless fine sand and outcroppings of jagged rocks that jut far into the ocean. The water feeds the people as much as the land does, as it yields an abundance of sea life that is harvested by blackened men with rough hands, keen eyes, and slight, but powerful, bodies. Time stands still in this part of the world, and there is a measure of outer peace and quiet that is unknown to the busy, noisy and hectic goings-on in the bigger cities a hundred miles away. Yet, somehow people have managed a way to create suffering, struggle, and pain where only paradise should reign. As such, it is the same everywhere, and like the harsh rays of the summer sun, this fact of life, too, seems oppressive and inescapable.

    I was born into a small family where we all dwelled in a thatch-roofed, two-room house on the outskirts of a dense jungle, and a short walking distance to the ocean. During the hottest times of year, my mother would cook outdoors, as would every other mother in the village. Except for sleeping and eating, very little else took place inside our tiny abode. While my mother tended our house and busied herself with raising my older brother and I, my father caught and sold fish for his livelihood. His life revolved around early morning forays out to sea in his small boat, accompanied by his helper, a fit but elderly gentleman who lived a stone's throw away from us.

Just before noon, my father would return with his catch and bring it to a man who would then prepare the fish for market, load it into his wagon, and head for the nearest town where the square was always bustling with impatient, shouting buyers. On occasion, due to inclement weather or some other unforeseen situation, my father would return in the afternoon with an empty boat. Sometimes this could go on for an entire week or two, and in response, a predictable panic would take place at home for fear of starvation and poverty.

"That's it!" my mother told my father during more than one such occurrence. "Put on a clean shirt. We are visiting the priest. It is up to the gods to save us from ruin. Clean yourself up and get the children. We are going without delay."

Rolling his eyes at my mother's dramatic display, my father began to argue: "This again? We have no money as it is, and now you want to pay that fool to save us from too few fish in the sea?"

"Mind your tongue!" my mother shouted at him. "You do not attack the priest, and you must not doubt his powers. See if it helps! See for yourself and you will find out who is the fool."

For all the insanity and fear bound up in my mother's method of paying for penitence, her plan nevertheless seemed to work time and again. Eventually fishing would be good again for my father, we would be saved from starvation, and the tension at home would be relieved. All would be forgotten until the next time, and then the cycle would repeat itself — and it always did.

My father took no solace in religion, but religion was alive in my mother and in our culture, so there was no avoiding its outstretched arms and its intrusion from everyone around us. Periodically, owing to my mother's religious devotion, rituals, prayers, and observances were thrust upon me and my brother, as they were on other children I had known. The only thing that kept us from being crushed beneath the thumb of the priesthood was my father's disinterest in religious matters of all sorts. His only apparent connection to a higher being was made known only when his business met with difficulty, the roof began to leak, his bicycle tire flattened, his boat sprang a leak, the changing tides had caused a poor yield from the sea, and those sorts of things for which he cursed the gods. I do not know whether it was from watching my father's disinterest and scoffing at all matters that were religious, but for me as well, religion cast no spell.

"If you do not follow the teachings," my mother would threaten my brother and I, "then your life will be of no use. Look at your father's indifference and see how he struggles. You will see the meaning of what it is to be cursed. All you need to know is provided for you; thinking beyond this will only get you into trouble."

There was no arguing with her.

My mother's enthusiasm for the unseen world and faith in a dizzying panoply of gods and spirits more than made up for my father's indifference. She was observant, superstitious, and outwardly pious. She lived in fear yet called it love. Unabashedly, she put on a good show of her devotion, dragging the family to every holiday celebration, and lighting an array of candles at altars she had strategically placed around the house. She even managed to make a competition out of religion, often baking and cooking for days on end so that she could throw the best observances in the village.

"Now we are feeding all the neighbors?" my father would holler at my mother.

"You will thank me when the light shines down upon us!" she would shout back at him while stretching her arms and hands toward the heavens.

"That would be nice. I've been waiting all my life," my father would say with great irreverence.

My mother felt pity for my father in his mockery of prayer. Regardless of my father's derision for her beliefs, or her fear of impoverishment now and then, she never thought twice about spending even her last savings as a display of her religious devotion. Twice a year at least, she would open our house to the neighbors after cooking up an array of dishes for religious observances. But behind the scenes it was apparent that she had no way of separating her piousness from her vanity. She relished compliments on her generosity and cooking skills, which were sure to come as villagers marched in and out of our house like a trail of ants carrying food away to their nests.

In the wake of the dirty dishes, soiled pots, and other mess, my older brother and I were assigned to clean up as my mother basked in her glory and my father scratched his head, wondering how hard he would have to work to pay for the madness.

My brother remained indifferent and did as he was told. He never questioned anything in life. Neither was he much bothered by the disposition of either of my parents. Unlike me, he had no aversion to public gatherings, my mother's showiness, or my father's forceful manner. And, he was content to work hard in hopes of one day having his own family and carrying on the tradition of trading labor for material gain. Although he had no personal interest in religious matters, he was anyway eager to help my mother in her eternal quest to gain favor with the priests, spirits, and gods. He did not think much beyond this, and, though he and I usually got along, he could not understand my need for answers to life's most difficult questions.

"You waste your time thinking about stupid things, do you know that?" he said to me on more than one occasion. "Who cares where we come from or the damn purpose of life? We are here, and we have to fight and scrape to make a go of it. You spend so much time with your thoughts somewhere else that one day you're going to smash your head into pieces from not paying attention."

I wondered if he was right to some extent. But I could not help myself. Life simply made no sense to me, and that included the words and deeds of most people.

Aside from these familial quirks, my upbringing and life were quite ordinary, I suppose, when compared with the lives of other children. I walked to school in the morning with my brother, played in the afternoons with friends along the beach, ate dinner with my family at the end of the day, went to sleep in the early evening, and repeated the whole cycle the next day. Such a lifestyle was sufficient for everyone around me, though I had often wondered whether there was a purpose to any of it. It all seemed so mechanical, hopeless, and meaningless to me, yet when I looked around I could see that everyone else simply accepted without questioning the struggles and monotony that confined and consumed them. People suffered, complained, prayed, cried, praised the gods when their fortunes improved, huddled in fear, and rejoiced at celebrations, but no one seemed interested in getting out from under this unending wheel of ups and downs and pleasure and pain.

As a child I had been uninvolved with financial woes, petty jealousies, strong differences of opinions, and other sorts of conflict, though I was aware of them just the same. The adults around me exhibited every emotion that was described in the religious texts — jealousy, envy, greed, anger, attachment to what little they had, gluttony, vanity, and the rest of them. Like my parents, our neighbors and friends had very little in the way of material possessions, but somehow found a way to take pride in them, and to worry about losing them. Their little problems were somehow regarded as monstrous, and these conflicts consumed them in myriad ways.

It seemed to me that the perpetual desire to have more, and to never be satisfied, was a sad state, though I had no idea whether this was avoidable. And, seeing a self-perpetuating cycle of pain and pleasure, I could never see the point in arguing, fighting, and scheming to obtain or retain possessions. And so I grew to be tortured by thoughts about the meaninglessness of life itself. Suffering caused me to suffer.

I must admit there were times when I turned to the religious texts in search of greater meaning, but when I had on occasions sat before the priests as they conducted their rituals, I found nothing more than blind faith and passionless words. The truth about existence — whether there was a meaning to life itself — seemed never to be discussed either by the priests or at home.   So what purpose did they serve?

Their message was that of "have faith and believe," which I found more than dissatisfying and dismissive. Throughout my youth I remained spiritually hungry, but did not fully know what it was that I was hungry for.

Due to my own opinions and values, I could never understand what it was that my mother found so alluring about the business of priests and religious rituals when she had no true interest in knowing anything about the Truth about life itself. Instead, she was forever playing what I had long considered an empty game of pretense. Her life consisted of bargaining for this and that — for forgiveness and for good luck, for money and to avoid pain. What she called praying I called begging. She could talk to god, but could not listen.

I once heard my mother ask my father, "Why is this our lot? Look at my friends with their merchant husbands. The men go away for a month and then return with jewelry, clothes, and nice things. What do I get from you? What do we have to speak of?"

My father would argue back, but my mother's words cut deeply into him, ever increasing his feelings of inferiority and anger.

"Don't you see what is going on?" my father once said. "What kinds of friends are these? They wait until enough people gather around in the market, and then they flaunt what they've purchased with their hard-earned money so that everyone can be a party to their extravagance. I give you all I can give, but it's never enough, is it?"

No, it was never enough. My mother tried to compete with her friends, as she spent too much money on dressing my brother and I for school so that the other mothers could see how we looked compared to the less fortunate (or more frugal) who arrived barefoot and tattered. My mother also took great pride in the way she dressed, cooked, and attended to her own beauty. She needed to look good to others, and even went out of her way to help the less fortunate, but only if her friends were certain to find out that she had done so. She called her work altruism and would cite the value of her giving from the religious texts, but I was always suspicious about her motives. Of course, I never told her so. All the while, at home, we seemed ever beset by some problem that wisely-saved money would have addressed — a leaky roof, cooking utensils that had long ago fallen apart, a scarcity of food, a wagon in disrepair, a cracked stove, several holes in the walls, my father's thread-bear fishing nets, and an array of broken-down necessities.

Often, on thick summer evenings, my mother and father would sit outside on our porch as my brother and I squirmed uncomfortably on our mattresses, unable to sleep from the hot, muggy air. We would listen to our parents talk for hours, frequently becoming embroiled in arguments about money.

My father's complaint was unchanging. He would say, "I'm always struggling, and you don't see it. Life would be a whole lot easier if you would only stop spending so much on frivolities."

Other times, fed up with his problems and the weight of his responsibilities, regardless of the cause, my father threatened to walk out on my mother, leaving her to her own devices. Crying, my mother would insist that nothing she did was frivolous, because she was giving to our family and community from her heart, as an outpouring of love.

"I spend money only for one reason," my mother would say. "I feed the neighbors according to the scriptures. We must do what we can, because it is our responsibility to provide for the poor."

After saying this, she would press her palms together and close her eyes as if in communion with god. This usually did the trick, as it appealed to my father's guilt. In the end, he refused to admit to himself that the source of her spending was her own vanity. His unending acquiescence hinged always upon his ultimate attachment to my mother who had provided him with some semblance of stability and a home life that barely slaked his insecurities yet represented some impression of normalcy in society. On and on this pattern cycled throughout my childhood years — flare-ups between my parents that quickly resolved themselves so that life could return to normal. Hope kept them going — hoping for more money, good weather, the favor of the gods, children who could make them proud, good health, grandchildren, and on and on.

It did not take a trained psychologist to see that my father carried around a lot of anger. His was not an easy life, and his upbringing with his own parents had left him empty and alone. In his developing years, they had never expressed their affection for him or his sisters. As soon as he had reached adulthood, he no longer could tolerate his family dynamics and, risking to forever become a pariah, he deserted them. At the age of seventeen, he set out wandering southward from home, for weeks on end, until discovering our little village by the sea where my mother and her family had lived for all their lives. My parents were introduced through a mutual friend, and a marriage was quickly arranged.

My father fell in love, as did my mother, with the idea of marriage and having their own family. Both were in search of independence from their families, and both were willingly jumping into a state of codependence.

Still, my father could never shake the anger that boiled at all times inside of him owing to his stressful upbringing and adversarial outlook. While my father was usually good about controlling his anger, there were times when he would scream and throw things at my brother and me for the most unreasonable reasons. If we were to accidentally wake him up from his afternoon nap, we would be on the receiving end of a tirade. It was not unusual, either, to see him go into a rage while frustrated with tangled fishing nets or a broken winch. I once saw him nearly come to blows with another man who had uttered a few words that my father misheard as a personal insult. If the other fishermen had not intervened, the result would surely have been bloodshed, or worse. While my father often could be warm and loving, he could just as easily fly into a rage at the slightest provocation, either real or imagined. I had always wondered whether he could see his own self-conflict, yet I never dared to speak with him about such things.

I had always admired my father's physical strength, however. He was not a tall man, but he was fit and muscular as a result of so many years of difficult feats of physical labor that few other men were willing or able to endure. He was also forceful and intimidating, but I was too young to understand that this trait was no more than a symptom of something deeper. He would throw things when he became frustrated, curse at the ineptitude of others around him, and yell at my brother and me for any infraction that a child is guaranteed to make. Ironically, and seemingly in contradiction to my father's bravado, I would eventually come to see that he was full of fear, for what else could explain his unending need to lash out at every turn? What was he trying to protect? I saw his volatility like that of a cornered wild animal.

My father's fears seeped into my brother and me in a variety of ways. He always seemed to be warning us against one potential danger or another, and his advice for us to stay safe knew no bounds. Be careful of the tides, he would say. Do not wander too near the jungle. Do not climb too high in the trees. Do not trust others, because they will always betray you. Don't let others get away with getting you to do something you do not want to do. Everyone wants something from you, so beware of their motives. A few of his warnings were practical, but most were his own fears projected onto us.

My father's anger became a hallmark of my own interactions and thoughts. I seem to have had inherited this burdensome emotion from him as a natural response to my problems, even at an early age. One day in school, the teacher gave us supplies to make a piece of artwork. Though I tried repeatedly to do so, I could not draw onto paper the images that were in my head, so I crumpled up the paper, threw it down, broke my pencils, and stormed out of the classroom. Another time, when I was out with my friends, we had a stick and a lopsided ball, and we were playing along the beach, lost in our own silliness. Then my older brother came to fetch me.

"Come home right this minute!" he demanded. I tried to ignore him, then he yelled, "Dinner is waiting. Mother says to come now. No more playing!"

I did not want to leave the fun of my game, but my brother insisted, and we got into a heated argument.

"No!" I shouted at him. "I'm in control of my own life. I will come home when I feel like it."

"You think so?" he yelled back at me.

He came toward me and I threw the stick at him, striking him in the foot. Without regard for the pain he was now in, he pounced on me and held my face down in the sand as I screamed like a wild animal before he finally got off of me and walked home. I reluctantly followed him, tethered to an invisible chain while seething with rage at him, my mother, and the unfairness of the world.

These now seem like trivial events, but it did not take much to rile my anger or frustrate me. And life grew more and more enraging to me with every passing year, so that I wanted nothing more than to be left alone. I hated everything — school, other children, my family, most of the villagers, and the home in which I lived. I felt trapped by the unfairness and senselessness that was life itself. I was not my own person, knew no peace or privacy, and I had no way to escape my own sense of self.

The rage inside of me continued to burn on and on throughout my childhood.

One morning my mother found me at the beach as I sat alone staring out at the waves. I was surprised to see her walking toward me, and when I first set eyes upon her, the peace inside me evaporated and I felt sick to my stomach. I nervously stood up as she marched up to me.

"Go and get washed," she commanded me.

I stared at her for a moment, feeling anger stirring within me as a response to her intrusion. I tried to answer carefully, but the words just spewed out of me.

"I am just trying to be by myself; I want to be alone," I said calmly.

"Alone?" she scoffed. "What do you do all day that you deserve leisure? Do you think you have things so hard that you can demand to do what you want? Does your father go off and sit under a tree? Your brother? Me? What a laugh! I told you to go and get washed. Go now!"

She pointed her finger and put a hand on her hip. Her face was stern, and her lips pursed.

"No," I said. Then I defiantly sat back down on the sand, buckled my hands around my knees, and stared out at the water.

"Don't play stubborn with me!" she shouted.

"I hate it," I said. "I hate it all. You drag us off to your stupid religious ceremonies, you make me sit with your friends and their stupid children, and you never listen to me," I said with a shaking voice.

"You have no right," my mother said. "No right. I will tell you what is best for you. You want me to listen to you? Yes, I want to listen to you say your prayers and do what is expected. Who are you to decide what is right for you? Now get up from this beach and march back home. We are going to the priest, and you are going to ask to be forgiven for your insolence."

I gave up resisting and, with rounded shoulders, walked back home to do as my mother commanded. Though I was several steps ahead of her I said, "You have no idea what is in my head or what my feelings are. You think you can force me to believe in your nonsense, but you cannot control my mind. You and your idiotic religion and your friends have nothing to do with me."

I prepared to be slapped, but my mother did no such thing. Instead she quietly followed me home, and in another hour we were standing in front of a shrine as I watched her light candles and mumble prayers to a deity I could not see. This was insane to me that my mother cared so much about trying to appease her gods and pray for goodwill and material possessions while completely invalidating her own son's pain.

On the rare occasions that I would try to talk to my father about my frustrations, he was either too angry himself to listen, or he would listen for a few minutes and then seem to quickly forget everything I had said in order to pacify my mother. In my pre-teen years, my frustration often led me to cry myself to sleep and plead to no one to show me a way out of my suffering.

The last straw

As the years passed, I found myself disinterested in life in general. I had no desire to achieve anything, nor did I care to participate in any social events. School was boring and seemed unnecessary. Because I was predisposed to complain about family outings, it got to the point where my parents stopped taking me along with them to their various excursions and celebrations so that I was left at home by myself. Occasionally they would return with a small gift for me, but I really had no interest in anything that most people considered to be of value.

When I reached the end of my teenage years and was still in school, my father insisted that I begin to learn his trade one day out of each weekend. I immediately discovered that I would never be able to survive if I had to endure this type of onerous work for the rest of my life. While sitting in his fishing boat on a calm morning, I decided to express my feelings to my father.

"I think I need something different," I told him.

While he was cutting a knot out of a fishing line, my father paused and looked out into the distance. Then he began again to saw away at the knot. He told me, "Life is very difficult, you know. It has always been this way. We want things, but we must work for them. We have obligations, and that is the way things are. So how do we get these things? We use our willpower and forge ahead. No one is going to do it for you. Persistence wears down resistance."

"But what if you are wrong? What if you and mother are going about this the wrong way? I watch you struggle and complain, but nothing changes," I said. "Nothing has changed for years."

"Of course we struggle. Struggle is what life is. If you expect happiness, then you will be sorely disappointed." He pointed his knife at the sky and said, "If you expect happiness, the result will be more unhappiness. You see how this is?"

Just then a small school of fish made its way into my father's nets and they swished around in the water.

"If nothing changes, and the struggling is just something that you have to accept, then why bother to complain all the time?" I shot back. "How can you have any hope?"

My father pulled on his nets to trap the fish as a trace of a smile rose across his face.

Sitting in that rickety old boat, I felt like one of the fish caught in the nets, looking for an escape from every possible angle.

"It doesn't seem right that we are here just to be unhappy most of the time," I said hesitantly.

"It's not right to you, because you don't know any better," my father said. "It is what it is. What is the use of all the talk?"

That conversation left me thinking. Although my hands and body may have been engaged in fishing with my father, my mind was completely occupied with the meaning of life. I recognized that there had always been a dim light inside of me that needed to find salvation, and now this light was beginning to burn more brightly. And this wasn't the kind of salvation that so many are seeking. I wasn't looking for a way out or to make life better. I could not be appeased by priestly promises or the salve of rituals mumbled into the air. It was more personal, and less tangible. I needed to know what was at the bottom of all the insanity, behind the suffering, beneath the hardships and rhetoric. Who would be able to point me to this Truth that I sought?

Three months later, on one very usual Saturday morning, I watched my family walk off toward the market, leaving me behind for the day. The rainy season had just ended, and the tiny crack that had appeared in my consciousness was about to widen with a small experience that would propel me to the next step. Bored and pent up, I walked to the beach and found a healthy coconut tree with dozens of thick, shady fronds to sit beneath. I stared up at the tree for a moment in awe of how such heavy fruit could hold on against the force of gravity calling it to the ground.

Tentatively, I positioned myself at the base of the tree, trying to find the safest spot should one of those coconuts come hurling off its purchase.

I pushed my feet under the warm sand and stared out at the ocean. My thoughts returned to the question of why I was alive, and I considered for a moment what it might be like if I was not.

I drew in a deep breath and closed my eyes so that now the sun was filtering in through red-orange eyelids. I knew that my world was marked by pangs of hopelessness, and life held no promise or meaning for me. I tried to shut out feelings of despair, to quiet my mind, but soon I was besieged by the usual thoughts. I declared to myself that I wanted nothing from this life except to know the Truth. Without this, I would no longer be able to bear the useless, senseless, monotonous, unrewarding life that I knew. I found myself talking to the world, airing my grievances, and praying for some sort of guidance. I did not believe there was a god to help me, so my prayers were unspecific and unfocused. I asked for no more than direction. My deepest wish could be reduced to two selfish words, "Help me," though I had no expectations of being helped in the least. To whom was I praying?

I opened my eyes to see thick, dark clouds gathering over the ocean. Somewhere far in the distance, the rain poured in torrents, and lightning flashed for several minutes before dissipating, so that the storm would never reach the shore. I listened intently to the ocean waves washing against the beach, and then I turned my face to a slight breeze that refreshed me yet failed to uplift my spirits. This was a beautiful morning, but I could not see the beauty in it. I felt myself to be a prisoner of my circumstances and my mind.

Consumed with emptiness, even my fruitless inner dialog came to a halt. Now and again, a solitary bird would swoop low over the water's edge, run along in search of food, find nothing, and then take flight again. Fifty yards out at sea, a pair of small fishing boats bobbed up and down in the surf, and the voices of the fishermen crackled intermittently in the air. I laid down on my back and exhaled, too sad and mentally exhausted to think.

It was at this moment that the sun came out from behind a cloud, and I was forced to close my eyes to shield out the intense light. My attention turned inward, and I dove into my own unhappiness. Already spent from sulking, I was moved to watch the part of myself that had bothered me for so long. Which part of me was so unhappy, I wondered. Then a thought occurred to me, one that prompted me to ask myself who could possibly know this answer. I questioned whether it was even possible to find out.

For a quick instant, I admitted to no one but myself that I did not know who I was, aside from all that ailed me. It seemed as if there were two of me held within the same being — the one who suffered and the one who knew that the suffering existed. I called the latter "me" the watcher. It had always been with me, always taking note of my every emotion, tantrum, and action — even in the heat of my anger, sadness, or despair. It was aware of me, aware of my hopelessness. I did not know what to make of this, and there was no one with whom I could speak of such things. This watcher was the true "me" through all of the ups and downs of my life.

I pulled myself out of the sand and sat upright, uncomfortably against the rough bark of the coconut tree. I was enveloped in an inextricable heaviness borne of the impossibility of understanding life and its absence of any sense. I stared blankly at the water washing up on the sand, and I reflected that there had always existed an undercurrent of sorrow within me. At times this pain was as palpable as the discomfort of my back against the weathered tree. I could feel the pain in my heart, in my nerves, in my stomach, and in my head. Even during the most joyous occasions, this sorrow had managed to erode the ground beneath all other emotions, events, and people. I knew myself to be this sorrow, yet there seemed to be no way of avoiding sinking further and further into it as the years rolled by. Discontent, unhappiness, depression, sadness, anger, and hopelessness marked my waking hours and haunted my dreams.

I thought about this sorrow for a long time until I understood that it was beckoning me to know myself. For some reason, I did not want to quell it, ignore it, or make it feel better. I invited it in. I listened to it, and I put my full attention upon it, in the same way that I would so often dispassionately watch the waves sneak up on the shore and then recede, over and over again. I looked at the minutia and the big picture, and I came to realize that I *was* the sorrow itself. The sorrow and this "I" was the same entity. I also realized that I was the *need* to know myself. I found myself embracing this desire and feeling it to the depths of my being. And then I resigned myself to finding out who it was that was doing anything at all, whether watching the gentleness of the sea or witnessing the sadness that comprised me. Who was I?

Sitting for hours as the ocean lulled me into a deep meditation, I had become completely lost in the silence behind my thoughts. I wondered whether I had fallen asleep, yet I remained aware. At times, all sound completely disappeared, even the rumble of the ocean, but at the instant I took notice, the sound of the waves, birds, and wind would return. I washed in and out of this state of nonexistence, at times losing all sense of the body. Absorbed in this meditation, I hardly noticed when two elderly men came dragging their feet through the quiet sand. It was only when they began to speak that I opened my eyes and looked at them.

The older of the two men had a difficult time walking on the soft beach, and so he paused every now and then to rest. Presently, he latched onto the arm of his friend, and they stopped to rest right in front of me, taking no notice of me at all. They launched into a lively discussion and were nearly shouting to hear themselves above the ocean. The younger of the two mentioned the teachings of a sage who lived in some far off place. He said that people from all over had visited this guru in some ashram far to the south, seeking to find their own true nature. The older man, hard of hearing, asked his friend to repeat the name of this sage, which he did. Upon hearing the name, the man laughed and waved off his friend in an act of dismissal. He said that he had heard of this guru, but suspected that the teachings were without much merit because they were simple and unimpressive.

"I would not waste my time with this nonsense," he said. "Everybody is looking to escape the world, and then gurus of this sort tell you that life is an illusion. What good does that do?"

"I don't know that you are getting it right," explained his friend. "We buy into the illusion; that's the main thing where everything goes wrong. The mind causes suffering because it desires. I can see that."

"So now you are Buddha? Please. And while we're at it — this guru you're talking about — I have been to that ashram. It's a small place with a little yard and people milling about. I have been to many ashrams, and this is the smallest. It's not even a dot on the map."

He went on to say that this sage of whom his friend was speaking had far fewer adherents than any other.

"Well," said the younger one with a chuckle, "that's really some strange way to appraise a spiritual teacher, don't you think? The ashram is too small, there are too few devotees. The next thing you'll say is that the food is not seasoned to your liking."

"What sort of fool would travel hundreds of kilometers to kiss the feet of a second-rate guru?" the older man continued. "If you want to know the meaning of life, it's this: You are born, you die, and then you are reborn. On and on it goes. Who needs a guru in some far off place to discover such a thing? I'll save you the trip and you can kiss *my* feet instead!"

Both of the men broke into laughter, then the older one started up again, saying that the guru seemed more interested in talking about the workings of the suffering mind than providing any solid answers for their problems. His companion shrugged his shoulders and then changed the topic of conversation. Then the pair renewed their walk up the beach.

With their departure, the name of this sage had lodged somewhere in my brain. I stood up and brushed the sand from my legs. As I began to pace back and forth, all my thoughts of self-loathing had now been supplanted by thoughts about this guru who was waiting for me in some far off land. I had decided to place my hopes in this stranger who could possibly relieve my sorrow. I had to find the guru; I had to find the Truth.

A week or so later, on the way to school, I asked my brother whether he had heard of this holy man of whom the old men had spoken so irreverently, and he said no, then asked why I had any interest. I tentatively asked him if he had ever wondered what the whole meaning of existence was.

"Why are we here?" I asked him. "Have you ever wondered?"

My brother shook his head then rolled his eyes. He wrapped his arm around my shoulder and we wobbled up the road together.

"Do you think you are the first to ask such stupid questions?" he said. "Or maybe you think your problems are more important than everyone else's. Who has time for such nonsense?"

My brother said that he had no interest in such matters. He said these kinds of issues only held meaning to priests and dreamers, but that I should be more concerned with finding a way to study harder in school then set my sights on making a living. Then he pushed me away and stopped in his tracks to tell me that the next reasonable step after this would be to find some girl to marry so that I could start a family.

"That's what I'm working on," he said with a smile. "A wife and my own house. You should be thinking of this instead of filling your head with stupid ideas that nobody has any answers to."

My brother suggested that the consequences of not heeding his advice might lead to my living as a worthless beggar combing the streets for scraps of food.

"For heaven's sake," he said, "take your head out of the sand. Make your family proud and grow up. What have you got to brood about, anyway?"

My brother's opinions, though somewhat predictable, served to reinforce my view that I was alone in this world and that perhaps it was futile for me to talk about things that seemed never to cross most people's minds. I paused for a moment to search my thoughts for anyone who could possibly entertain questions that seemed to have no answers. There was no one I knew personally.

From that day forward I stopped asking my brother about matters that seemed only to concern me. I also knew better than to ask either my mother or father, sure that their answers would be even less validating than those of my brother. The idea that I was without a mentor depressed and angered me at the same time.

When the weekend rolled around, to the pleasant surprise of my mother, I decided to go with my family to the next village where we were going to watch a renowned holy man lead a special religious ceremony. Because her friends from around the village would be in attendance, my mother was excited about making a grand entrance, and when I said I wanted to go along, she was greatly encouraged that I was at long last showing an interest in religious matters.

"I knew you would come around," my smiling mother told me while rocking up on her toes and holding her folded fingers to her lips. A couple of days later she presented me with a new shirt for the occasion.

My mother's joy was contagious, and we both shared a passing elation over the prospects of our family excursion. I tried on my mother's gift, and as I was buttoning up, she helped straighten my collar and said that she was proud of me. I told her that I loved her, and she ran her fingers through my hair but was too choked up to speak. She nodded and smiled through her tears.

It took an hour of walking until we reached the town square. It was overflowing with visitors from every surrounding village. The intoxicating odors of food cooking on open cauldrons saturated the air, and there was the indistinct din of hundreds of human beings chattering away with hardly anything of importance to say. My mother dragged us around to her friends and proudly introduced us.

"These are my sons," she said a little too boisterously. "It's so difficult to dress them in the best clothes, you know.

Things are so expensive these days. But what can you do if you have to have the best, right?"

Though my mother's friends were showing signs of boredom, with a laugh she also hinted around that we were open for offers if anyone had a daughter or two whom they needed to marry off. My brother smiled politely and waggled his eyebrows, but I remained uncomfortable all through a string of these vapid conversations that repeated themselves a half dozen times over the next couple of hours. My father, too, longed to escape from the vacuous interactions with so many strangers.

And then the ceremony began. The priest and his acolyte made a great show for the people who stared up at them with religious awe. After the priest blessed his flock while letting his hands float skyward, and the ceremony came to a close, I cautiously approached him and waited patiently behind a couple of his devotees for my turn to ask him a question. Then an older woman pushed her way in front of me so she could petition the holy man to bless her son. This aroused a bit of anger in me, and I tried to protest, but she kept her back to me and fawned all over the priest.

While waiting my turn to speak, I studied the priest as a source of wonder, noticing several expensive rings on his fingers, and a chain of gold about his neck. His robe was so clean and bright that the morning sun reflected off of it like some large sail out at sea. It was pressed so that not one errant crease or wrinkle interrupted the way it draped over his well-fed belly. I focused on the priest's toothy mouth as clever words rolled seamlessly off his lips. He had a gift for speech, always saying the right thing that put his followers in their place, and they never dared to question his wisdom or authority. I watched his well-manicured fingers find a place to rest on a man's shoulder as a show of affection before he suggested working at the local temple as a means of saving the man from failure in business.

At last it was my turn. I was now standing beside the holy man, as a throng of people hung on his every word for a scrap of wisdom that would uplift them out of their dull existences. I somehow expected to receive an electric feeling, or some sort of powerful energy from the man. Yet there was no such experience. In fact, the longer I stood waiting my turn, the priest began to seem less holy to me, and my instincts told me to turn around and abandon the idea of conversing with him. But this I did not do. Instead, when our eyes met, I forced a smile and he responded in kind and then pulled me to him so that we were face-to-face at hardly arms' distance.

"Do not be bashful," he said while turning his attention to an attractive young woman passing by, "Ask your question."

Then he looked at me, grabbed onto my forearm and pulled me even closer. I cleared my throat, then nervously asked whether there was a purpose to life.

"Living and dying, over and over again, seems absurd to me," I told him. "You have talked about reincarnation and karma, but what about *this* life that we are now living? What does it mean? What is the purpose of all the suffering? It's all I see. How can you prove any of the things you say about how we should live a pious existence?"

Though I was taller than him, he responded by looking down his nose at me before letting out a derisive chuckle. He laid his heavy hand on my shoulder and dug in with his fingers until it was quite uncomfortable. The priest softly told me that I should never be asking such questions unless I wanted to invoke the wrath of the gods.

Then he said with a booming voice that lifted me off my feet, "Who are you to question anything, boy?"

His words were loud enough for all to hear. I sensed that his goal was to make a spectacle of me, and I quickly grew humiliated. His eyes darted around to connect with his audience. Several others who were waiting for their turn for a blessing joined in and laughed at me. A cold chill ran up the back of my neck. I recognized a familiar, ever-present anger beginning to rise within me, yet I managed to control it. I then asked the priest why I might meet with such wrathful consequences if my questions came from a sincere desire to know.

"If you and the gods have any interest in helping people, then you would have some good answers, and life would not be so full of suffering and hardship. Why do you dismiss me, or is it that you do not know everything as you pretend to?"

Not used to being challenged, the priest was now visibly annoyed with me and responded without saying a word. With a scowl and a grunt, he turned his back to me, completely ignoring my existence. Though I was embarrassed, I was now even more angry, and again I resisted the inclination to walk away. I was feeling not only bothered and abused, but demanded at least a modicum of respect.

As the priest began bestowing one of his devotees with his sage advice on the complications of marriage and family life, I interrupted and persisted with my questioning. Anger and frustration continued to well up in me, on par with his unwillingness to help me. I asked the priest again why the gods would want to harm someone for asking a sincere question.

"Maybe I am right — the problem is that you do not know the answer to any of my questions," I said angrily. "What good do you serve if you can't answer me?" Then I pushed him too far, saying, "What sort of holy man are you if you have no answers to life's most basic questions?"

The priest aggressively turned toward me, utterly irritated, yet offered no answer. He tried to make his eyes bore a hole into me, and then he told me to go away before turning his back on me once again.

"Do you not have the answer?" I taunted the man. I tried to place myself in front of him so he would have to face me. "What kind of priest are you not to have such a simple answer? Who are you to call yourself a holy man? Answer me!"

At this point, I was no longer even interested in what he had to say, but more focused on venting my rage. The priest's eyebrows scrunched together and he clenched his jaw. He began to breathe heavily out of his nose.

"Go away, boy," he commanded in his deep voice. "Now!"

With my shoulders back and my head held high, I began to walk to the other end of the dais. The priest's insolence had set off a bomb in me, and without a second thought, I kicked over his table and sent its offerings, statues, pictures, food, and candles crashing in all directions. The sound of breaking glass shocked and surprised everyone in the area. Then I picked up a small statue and hurled it at the holy man, but he stepped aside just in time to avoid being struck. This immediately caused quite a scene as trinkets noisily continued to clank and roll away. In reaction, people started screaming curses at me as they scrambled after the clanging metal icons falling from the platform.

The priest took a couple of steps backward as I began to rush forward, ready to pounce on him. Then his assistant, like a referee in a heated match, pushed himself between us, grabbing me by the shirt to keep me from doing more harm. I heard the material tear and the buttons pop free as I twisted to get away. With his fists clenched, my father jumped up on the platform like a tiger, clearing all three steps and landing with a thunderous clap. He was coming to my defense, threatening to punch the next man who dared take a step forward. But with encouragement from their wives, the men began to close in on us. Now my brother, too, inserted himself into the fray, and just as a brawl was about to ensue, the holy man held his arms up to the heavens and shouted to his followers that no harm had been done.

"Stop! Stop! He's just a boy," the priest announced. "Just a boy who needs more attention from his mother and father. Please! There is no harm. Everyone calm down. Let us find the peace inside of us..."

Although the crowd immediately began to loosen up and back away, my father took the priest's words as a personal insult, and this made him even angrier so that it was now my mother who had to step forward to pull us away from the scene.

The priest again raised his hands to keep the crowd from stirring, and he proclaimed that the gods will take care of me and my family in their own way by imposing the appropriate measure of karma for our misdeeds.

I lacked the words to defend myself, and as I was pulled away by my brother, all I could do was glare back at the priest in all of his manicured pretentiousness. He stared back at me with a sickening grin, and I hated that he had won the fight as my mother, with her head held high, quickly led us all out of town and toward the safety of our village. Along the way, angry and embarrassed, she berated me for tearing my new shirt, as well as causing such a ruckus that made her look bad in front of her friends. Next she yelled at my father.

My mother cried, "Have you all gone mad? My friends...and the whole community...are probably laughing at us behind our backs. How do you expect me to show my face ever again? I am so embarrassed that I lack the words for it."

"Who cares?" my brother snapped back.

At this, my mother ran out in front of him, blocked him from taking another step forward, and then slapped him hard across the face, to the surprise of all of us. No other word was spoken among us until we returned home. Then my mother told me I would no longer be invited along with the family to any religious festivals. She said that I should be ashamed of myself and pray to the gods for forgiveness.

"How will I ever show my face again?" her voice crackled with shame.

I knew better than to offer a response, which would have resulted in an identical action to the one my brother had received. So I said nothing. I was no longer angry, and now I was seeing the world as if it were a play being enacted before me. Even I was a character in it, misbehaving, out of control, filled with rage, unhappy, and without a sense of belonging. And the priest was like one of those wicked characters from one of the traveling shows, designed to rile up the audience before an important moral lesson was delivered to make it all come out right in the end.

My long journey begins

What my mother considered to be a punishment — my banishment from all family outings — was actually a blessing to me. A year had quickly passed, and there was not one trip into town, nor one festival or religious ceremony that included me as a participant. Each time my mother took my brother and father on one of her excursions, I headed off in the opposite direction, making a ritual out of going to the beach. Once there, I would sit beneath the same coconut tree where I had made a mental note of the sage's name mentioned by the two elderly men on their stroll. That sage was now all I could think about.

As I settled down in my favorite spot, I clasped my hands around my knees and gazed out onto the agitated ocean. I breathed the sea air deep into my lungs, trying to relax. Though my family would be gone until dusk, I could not relieve the tension that I had carried with me to the beach. My mother, brother, and father were spending the day at a bazaar that was being held in conjunction with some religious holiday with which I was hardly familiar. But I knew that the real reason for the excursion was so that my brother could meet the family of a girl who had become a candidate for his wife. I knew that in another year or so I would be next, unable to escape the inevitable cementation of my life into someone else's dream.

Worried about what I might say or do, my decided not to expose the family to my ill manners until the deal had been sealed. My mother had my brother and father dressed exquisitely for the occasion. She had even made my father visit the barber for a fresh shave and haircut. Since sunup the previous day, my mother spent hour after hour baking sweets for the meeting before tutoring my father and brother on how to make a good impression.

During my family's absence, I hoped to treasure my solitude at the beach. It was a warm but breezy day, and I set out into the cool ocean for a swim. The water was refreshing and I stayed under the surface for as long as I could, trying to erase not only the outside world, but also the troubling thoughts that filled my head. After I came up for air I bounced up and down with the waves while staring back at the sandy shore. My life, I thought, was "over there," and I was here in the water, free of it for now.

The rhythm of the ocean was hypnotizing and soothing but it wasn't long before my mind fell onto my worldly problems and filled me with questions. As usual, I wondered what this life was for me, and why it seemed always to be so purposeless and troubling. How much longer could I live without any hope of finding an escape from a most mundane and meaningless existence? I took another deep breath before once again sinking to the sandy ocean floor beneath the waves. Now I could think of nothing and just lost myself in the silence. A minute later I had to come up for air, but now something had changed in me. An idea had come to me, filling me with excitement and pushing me toward my next move.

I marched out of the ocean, stared up at the sky, and then sat down on the hot sand, but my mind was racing and I had to get up and go. With a great deal of determination, I ran home, quickly gathered a few basic necessities in a little rucksack, along with some money I took from my parent's room, and I began to walk away from this little village that I had known since birth.

Just before I turned onto the main road leading south, I stopped, drew in a deep breath, then looked back. The whole scene was surreal and strange. Everything that had ever been familiar to me was suddenly new and changed. Was I really leaving? I told myself that I could easily turn around and return home; no one would know the difference. But I didn't. I glanced up at the branches high in the trees and listened to the sounds of the birds. I don't believe I had ever heard them before. Then I soaked in the surroundings, adjusted my rucksack, and bade my old life farewell.

I walked away at a brisk pace, leaving everything in hopes of finding the Truth about life. I was determined to somehow find the sage whose faceless image had for so long occupied my thoughts.

I traveled on foot for days on end, careful to remain on the main roads to avoid bandits that had been reported to attack travelers in the cover of night. Whether bandits had actually existed was not truly known, but I heard the voice of my father to keep alert and safe. I wanted to be brave, but my training kept me in a constant state of fear.

A few days passed quickly, and, despite having eaten nearly all my provisions and desperately needing sleep, I continued to push forward. Between the heat of the day and my relentless pace, my evenings were filled with dreamless deep sleep that left me refreshed enough to resume my travels just as the sun came up. On the fifth day, I arrived in a bustling town that was tremendous compared to the size and population of my home village. I began asking people about this sage whom I had set out to find. I mentioned the guru's name whenever I could in hopes of eliciting a promising answer, but no one in this place had heard of the man. I began to wonder whether I had misremembered his name, or whether the old men on the beach had mispronounced it. In any case, I had reached the point of no return. Since I could no longer live under my parents' roof in a life that was devoid of fulfillment, I stubbornly kept heading southward.

My travels had not in the least assuaged my anger or dissatisfaction with life, yet they did seem to burn off a lot of pent up energy. As I walked along, my mind still raced with thoughts, some mundane and others bothersome. For long stretches there was nothing but an empty dirt road ahead of me and weedy grasses flanking each side. An occasional tree shaded me for hardly a moment until I had passed from its shadow to the next one, but mostly there was nothing but a monotonous, unending landscape on the outside, and on the inside — in my head — there were heavy images of my family and a persistent longing to uncover the great Truth of life.

All manner of thoughts, unwanted and unshakable, remained my constant companion. Mostly they served to reinforce a sense of unhappiness within me. Also, I continued to carry with me the disturbing thoughts of my run-in with the priest that stirred up an anger on par with what I had experienced on the day it happened, complete with a quickening of my heartbeat and vengeful thoughts. My mind at times became consumed by a fantasy of pummeling the priest to exact some measure of justice to which I was entitled. But eventually these thoughts would give way to frustration that I had no control over my own untamed and violent mind. And after the frustration there was a return to silence. Over and over I watched my thoughts, and this became the preoccupation of my waking hours.

After trudging along for days at a time, weary and hungry, I eventually came to a healthy stand of trees overlooking a refreshing waterway on one side and a tea plantation on the other. I climbed up a tall banyan tree so I could peer out over the scenery. The infinity of the rich landscape gave me pause to think of my own insignificance.

I admitted to myself that I was lost, not just physically, but spiritually as well. I had been wandering with no plan or route, on only a thin hope that I would find what I thought I needed out of life — some holy man to bestow upon me the secrets of the universe.

From my perch high above the road, I looked in all directions. I could see the boring winding road that I had been traversing, and up ahead the scenery was much more inviting and picturesque — green, lush, and swept by a refreshing breeze that tickled the tall grasses and tree leaves.

I carefully climbed back down and rested for a few minutes in the shade. Despite the more welcoming view to come, I remained a stagnant, dark, dirty, mire of sadness. I sighed deeply, picked up my rucksack, and then continued on my way. The sorrow of life had begun to consume me again, leading me to thoughts of giving up, starving myself, and then laying down somewhere to die. Ironically, however, there arose in me a fear that would not allow this to happen. I thought of it as fear, but perhaps someone else would have called it an instinct to survive. Or maybe it was some form of hope. I could not tell. In any case, I picked up my pace, eager to experience a change of scenery.

I asked myself what it was that I was doing and where life was leading me, but I received no answer. I was unhappy sleeping under trees, begging for food, and nursing my sore and blistered feet by soaking them in rain puddles. And I had begun to stink without any means to cleanse myself. There was no way to avoid sweating profusely in the damp heat that marked every single day once the sun had risen overhead.

I decided to take a slight detour off the main road, and I made my way to a wide stream up ahead. I washed myself and my clothes as best as I could then sat beneath the shade of a tree to dry off. Feeling much refreshed, I rested for a little while and listened to the gurgling of the water over well-worn stones, and the birds chirping over my head. After an hour passed, I began to feel guilty about relaxing, so I got dressed and continued on my way.

By the end of the second week of chasing my dream, I came upon train tracks and followed them to a station where I discovered a wave of passengers disembarking and rushing to greet their relatives and friends. There was one small group of people who reminded me of my family, and a pang of homesickness grabbed me in the stomach. For a few moments I sat thinking about how my mother must have been worried about me, and what my selfish actions had done to her peace of mind. My father and brother must have set out to look for me, and I felt guilty about this as well.

I was so consumed with my own misery and guilt that I sat down on a bench, lowered my head between my knees and tried to regain my composure. That's when a young man about my age had taken a seat beside me. When the roar of excited train passengers had quieted down and the platform had nearly emptied, the fellow made a curious comment. He said that people were lost souls always looking for a place to be, and that the secret was to go within and find the master. I was much too tired, hungry and in need of another bath to engage in a philosophical conversation, so I tried to ignore him. He continued rambling on anyway until I looked up at him with a puzzled expression, which he considered an invitation to conversation. He told me that he too was once confused, but that he had found the ultimate truth. Why was he saying all of this to me?

I searched the young man's face for something that might tell me whether he could be trusted. I found no clue at all. He seemed friendly and confident, but my father's voice boomed in my head, telling me that everyone is selfish, and a fool is one who ignores his intuition and training.

The young man said that it seemed as though I could use a refreshing bath and something to eat. To that I could readily agree. He said he knew just the place, and he invited me to a water hole a mile or so away. Since my money had almost completely run out, and I was sorely in need of bathing, I followed him down the road, but with a measure of caution. As we walked along, I assessed the young man's physical stature. He was not as fit as I was, and I came to the conclusion that I could adequately defend myself should he attempt to assault me. Once more, my father's face popped into my thoughts and I grew very serious and prepared for a fight. I was beset with no other thoughts except those regarding how I might react if attacked. My heart began to race and my ears perked up at the prospect of such an encounter. There was even a measure of anger coursing through my veins. Was he showing me a kindness or was he leading me into a trap? I kept to the middle of the road just in case the man's accomplices were hiding in the trees. What would my father or my brother do in this situation? Now a different kind of thought flashed in my head, and I asked myself who it was that was so afraid of what could happen to me. I had no real time to explore this question, because my companion was given to unceasing chatter.

As we walked farther along, I carried on an inner dialog, rationalizing to myself that my cautious attitude was not borne of fear, but rather practicality. I had been taught that people were untrustworthy, self-centered, and prone to pushing others about. I wondered what this person had to gain by doing me a kindness, so I remained on guard as my companion made little jokes and treated me like an old friend. Somewhat surprisingly, in less than a half an hour, as he had promised, we came upon a large water tank where several others were happily bathing.

Large leafy trees lined the entire area, offering cool shade to the bathers. We left our belongings on the dry bank and jumped in the water. The temperature was refreshing, and we splashed around for so long that the skin on our fingers and toes had puckered. In the meantime, my acquaintance had taken the opportunity to tell me all about his religion in which anyone could use his power of thought to conjure up the image of the master. Just as I had suspected, there was an ulterior motive! For the pleasure of the bath, I was forced to listen to him rattle off what could have been a prepared sales pitch.

"We all have this power," the young man told me. "The inner master is real, and he has an outer form as well."

We are all souls, he said with great confidence, "sparks of God." Then, with our eyes closed, he led me through one of his contemplative exercises of imagination. With his encouragement I was able to see a figure in a light robe in my inner vision, and this made my new friend very happy, though I really had no idea what was going on.

"You see?" he said joyfully, "anyone can do it."

"What if I imagine a cow in a priest's robe?" I asked sardonically. "Does this mean that the cow is your spiritual master? How reliable is imagination anyway?"

"You can mock me if you like," he said with a grin, "but you must have faith or you will never get anywhere. Trust me, we were meant to meet one another today so I could show you the way to salvation."

Perhaps I was indeed mocking him, but my question was quite apropos to his suggestion that the imagination was the tool to find the ultimate Truth. To me, it was quite a faulty tool, and my young guru was more than naïve and gullible.

He proceeded to tell me that his master was the god-man who lived on many planes of existence and had come to this earth with the purpose of uplifting humanity. He said that his cult was based on soul travel, which was the ability to leave one's physical body and experience the wonders of being without the mind while traveling through the many inner worlds of existence.

"If you are aware of everything in this state," I said, "then how can you say that the mind is not involved?"

He stared at me for a moment, and then it became apparent that he had no answer. Then he cleared his throat and said, "It is a whole other reality; not this one of suffering."

"Do you still know who you are in this reality?" I asked.

"Of course," he said.

"Then the mind is the same, so what have you escaped?"

Again he fell silent.

Though I had a few times in my life experienced a strange presence of not being in my physical body, I was put off about my friend's cult and its leader. I failed to see how any of this had to do with knowing the ultimate Truth behind all of life, which is what I had been searching for. This business of using the imagination for conjuring up images seemed too complicated and simple-minded all at once. And it seemed unreliable to me. Something told me that the secret to life could not possibly be uncovered by playing with the imagination and fortifying the little sense of self via some sort of fantasy. This so-called teaching that my companion was so enthused about hinged on the power of the mind and a cult leader eager to lead his flock astray. I already felt that it was the mind itself that was the seat of all our problems. I could see this in my own thoughts without needing a teacher to tell me so.

"Without knowing the absolute Truth," I said, "life is meaningless, and we are all just wandering aimlessly and suffering."

"But this *is* the Truth," he said emphatically.

He told me to just believe in the master, because that was all one needed. Then he showed me a well-worn photograph of his god-man that he had carried with him at all times. I immediately thought of the priest who had infuriated me with his call for the gods of karma to punish me. A new thought jumped out at me, and it spewed forth in my father's voice.

"You cannot trust anyone, because everyone only wants something from you. This is a hard fact of life," I said. "Especially this man whom you've never met," I added. "For all you know he could be a charlatan of the highest order. You really know nothing at all about him or anything else. You're just a follower going on blind trust, and as proof of this man's power all you have is your own faulty imagination. Can I turn him into a duck by just imagining that he is a duck?"

I almost thought of asking the fellow what he wanted from me, but I decided not to. I settled down and decided to make peace after considering that at least he had made good his promise to lead me to a bath and share his lunch with me.

My companion shook his head in condescension, then enthusiastically said, "We have plenty of time to talk, but first thing's first. I'm going to help you find work."

A day later, he introduced me to his employer who owned a small but busy company that operated out of a dilapidated old building. Along with a handful of other laborers about my age, I spent long days loading heavy sacks of rice, peppers, spices, and flour onto outbound wagons. Along with my new coworkers I moved around inventory, swept the floors, and performed other laborious tasks from early in the morning until sundown. The pay was not bad, and it was fair and steady. I lived in a hut with my newfound friend and two others who worked for the same little company. I thought of my father and how he might have been proud of me for working hard and learning to be responsible.

Another breaking point

I had relatively few expenses, except for food and lodging, which enabled me to save most of my earnings in anticipation of eventually leaving my place of employment and continuing on my quest to find the sage whose name was etched into my mind. Still, it was as if I was caught in an undertow, an inertia that pacified the mind and body. Part of me felt I could continue living like this, because all my basic needs were being met and I owed nothing to anyone. But beneath this, something continued to stir in me, and I sensed a great stagnation consuming my young life. I was gently being pushed out the door. Still, I resisted giving up the security and freedom I had.

Days turned into weeks, and weeks into months, and life had become a habit. Compared to living on the highway, without a home or family, it felt good to at least have a place to sleep, regular meals, and physical work to occupy my thoughts. Even my body felt better, as my strength and endurance continued to increase from long days of arduous labor. But after nearly a year, the novelty was finally wearing off, and I was restless.

On a rare day at work, because we had not received our usual shipment from our supplier due to heavy rains, I sat alone in a filthy warehouse and contemplated my existence. With time to reflect, I had begun to resent myself for the drudgery that had become my life. Somehow, and quite insidiously, the feelings of emptiness I had left behind in my own village had manifested once again in my life. I was still lost, and still without purpose. People all around me still had problems, they were still petty, and they tried to slake their suffering with material goods and entertainment. What had changed for me except the scenery? Everyone was caught in a cycle without hope or end, and I felt I was being drawn further into a void of a worthless, painful existence.

I soon relapsed into an unshakable pattern of depression and anger, so much so that when my friend began one evening to pontificate about the wondrous teachings of his master, I was in no mood to listen. I was already agitated before he started in with his dogma. I was loathing my life and feared spending the rest of my days lugging around heavy sacks and engaging in the most vacuous conversations with fellow workers who were completely satisfied living like beasts of burden.

Returning from one of his monthly cult meetings to discuss the joys of his infallible master, my friend began to speak with an annoying pretense of wisdom and calm. I was physically spent from the day's work and had been contemplating my own state of unhappiness. I told him I did not want to hear any of his rants about god, his master, or his faulty opinions about the meaning of life. I told him I was tired of being pressured to join his, or any, belief system, and he needed to keep his thoughts to himself. But, oblivious to my sentiments, he began to lecture me about my need to overcome my poor temper and to surrender to his guru who was god-incarnate.

As far as I was concerned, my frustration and anger over my life was more real than any man claiming to be a gift from heaven, and now I was near the boiling point. Standing up to face him, I told my friend that I had hated being subjected to his dogma from the first day we met. I asked him why he thought he had the right to single me out for my shortcomings, and he told me that my use of the word "hate" was a sign of my spiritual immaturity. At that, I felt the muscles of my chest, back and arms begin to tighten, and I threatened him to mind his own business.

I was in no mood to hear stories of a self-proclaimed savior and his supposed powers to transcend this plane of reality. What did this have to do with me realizing the ultimate Truth about myself? I said that I did not invite my friend's criticism over something he called my spiritual capacity. I started for the door, fearing that I soon would not be able to control the anger that was inside of me, but my friend blocked the exit and persisted in his lecture. He responded to my objections by putting on an air of peaceful detachment and trying to humor me, but this, of course, only angered me even further. I ordered him to step aside, but he would not. As I stared at him, I realized that my very first impressions of him had been right all along. His ulterior motive had always been to manipulate me and try to recruit me into his little cult. Clearly, I thought, he was lost in a delusion of his own imagination. For one who spoke so often and expertly about the need to cultivate awareness, he was completely blind to my feelings. He now began talking about how his master protects all of his followers who surrender fully to his powers, and that all but the doubters and "outsiders' are brought into his aura.

"Salvation is yours if you would only believe," he told me.

"You know what you are?" I yelled at him. "You are a sorrowful person looking for magical experiences to boost your own sense of self. That's why you follow that ridiculous master of yours. With softly spoken words, he feeds you with the kind of wisdom that even a child can utter, and then he tells you that your imagination is reality as long as your thoughts are consumed with his glorification. He is a phony, but you are worse. You are a fool, and you want everyone else to be a fool as well. But," I said, "your type of fool is the worst, because you are trapped in an ignorance that you have no way to realize. At least I know that my own mind is my enemy. You, on the other hand, pretend that yours is your salvation. Now, get out of my way!"

He would not budge, and I could not stay still. I glared at him, but he acted unconcerned. Pacing around the room like a panther in a cage, I yelled at him to be quiet, but with no effect. Again I told him to get out of my way so I could leave, but he stood at the doorway and lectured me on how his experiences of meeting on "inner planes" with his master were real, and he said that it was only because I was of a lower consciousness that I could not yet know the wonders of the universe that came by accepting the master as my savior. That did it! I could take no more of his taunting. I burst into a rage, picked up a big clay bowl from the floor, and threw at him with all my might. It hit him on the shoulder then bounced off, shattering into pieces against the wall. So enraged was I that I wanted to kill him. I picked up a paring knife and I started toward him with fire in my eyes. At last he woke up and saw the monster that I had become. Wincing in pain from his bruised shoulder, he was now fearing for his life. He started to cower and pleaded for me not to hurt him.

"So much for protection and faith!" I screamed at him with the knife in my fist.

He backed all the way out the door and then quickly fled the hut. That was the last I would ever see of him.

Still seething, I quickly gathered what little belongings I had, as well my savings that I had hidden in the hollow bed railing, and I stormed off into the night. I did not know where I was going, but I knew that I had to keep moving or risk doing myself or someone else harm. All the while I was consumed with a familiar, unshakable rage, as well as hate for people in general.

For the next week or so, nearly everyone I encountered seemed to reconstitute my anger. The world for me had become a nasty, intrusive, harsh, and terrible place. I thought of people whom I had known over the course of my life, and felt that they had all wanted nothing more than to impose their beliefs on me — not just religious beliefs, but also their way of thinking and doing things. The inhabitants of this world are all self-involved and self-centered, I thought. I also recalled various people I had known who were followers of priests and gurus, hoping in some way to be uplifted and released from their burdens and suffering. How stupid they were! What did they do to deserve any sort of blessing? Everyone was a phony, pretending to be good whenever it suited them, but acting only according to self-interest at all other times. And their obsession with holy men and religion was some sort of game that I could never understand. Some had talked about gurus who could transmit their life essence into other people and enlighten them. Others said there were sages who could read their minds and make all their problems disappear at the snap of a finger or with the repetition of a mantra. Still others had teachers who pompously sat on a dais and pontificated to their gullible audiences about the evils they had attracted by way of karma.

There seemed to be so many gurus, but if their devotees were any indication, I doubted that they were making much of an impact on this world except to create a following for themselves while feeding the starving egos of their congregants.

I remained dissatisfied and empty as I walked southward. I placed my anger in my gait and covered great distances, never stopping for inclement weather and avoiding people whenever I could. All the while I lamented the fact that there were no answers to the most basic questions I yearned to have answered: Who was I, and was it even possible for me to find out? Who could help me? I doubted seriously that anyone could.

After another month had passed on the road, I had finally exhausted myself of a stream of hateful thoughts and fantasies of enacting revenge against everyone who had ever harmed me. In the most sober of moments I asked myself, if I had despised everyone so much, why would I still be interested in pursuing this guru who existed nowhere but as a conjured up image in my mind. Maybe it was all a bad idea, I considered. Was he even real? And if so, why wouldn't he just be like the rest of them? I had no answers and did not know what drove me on, other than a persistent, restless mind and spirit. But, this being my quest, to find one humble teacher who was interested in no more than the ultimate Truth, I vowed to myself that I would travel to the end of the earth to meet him. This was the only purpose to a sorrowful, angry life that was hanging by a thread.

The frustration of dealing with people and everyday worries and problems was the whole reason why I had left my family and village in the first place, and yet, since my departure I had faced the same problems, and suffered from the same emotions, wherever I went. On my journey I had watched strangers heatedly arguing with one another in marketplaces, and there were vain men of financial means staring down their noses at the less fortunate. There were mothers screaming at their children, and grandparents shaking their heads at the foolishness of the young. It's as if the same types of people were planted with seeds to grow in every corner of the earth. I saw the world as a strange, flowing river of sadness, anger, joy, jealousy, rage, laughter, tears, and greed. Happiness did not last, as it was always quickly supplanted by misery. Around and around it went, and almost no one seemed to care to end the cycle.

At times I would sit down on a large stone in the middle of the night and stare blankly at some body of water reflecting the moon. I thought to myself about how fitting a metaphor this was — the water was turbulent and ran deep, but sometimes on the surface there was a serenity that was impossible to comprehend. In this quiet I could see myself as a winding stream of phases and emotions. I did not like what I saw; I could not make it stop.

Since I had set foot on this journey, I had come to witness flaming balls of emotions and uncontrollable reactions repeated over and over again, regardless of the causes. It was so insane and stagnating, and I was somehow inseparable from it. Here and there I had considered throwing up my hands in resignation and returning home, but the more I had thought about the proposition, the more it depressed me. No, it would be much better to continue wandering through the countryside than to come up empty-handed without at least meeting this one guru.

And so I continued to walk and walk and walk.

Energized by the cooler temperatures, I came to find myself trekking through the nights, meditatively and quietly. I experienced absolute darkness under a cloudy sky that blocked out the moon and stars. And in that blackness I knew nothing of myself, unable to see even my hands before my eyes. Disembodied, I marched over beaten-down gravel paths, somehow keeping on the road by way of a concerted effort of my senses. Animals cried out and others growled and grumbled. I was alone with fear and sometimes awe and delight. On one occasion, well into the night, suddenly another traveler was right beside me, invisible in the darkness. His footsteps and breathing was all that I knew of him. His presence remained for an hour, silent and ghostlike.

He was a perfumed shadow that grunted out a greeting upon his arrival and then a one-word farewell before disintegrating into the blackness. After he had passed, I thought myself to be a shadow as well. I questioned my existence, and then my fate. Did I exist at all without sight or body? Who was I without the form, invisible not only to the world, but to myself as well. What did this make me? Who was I, then? Somehow I did not need a body or any other being to witness me in order for me to say, "I am."

I wondered whether I had ever been in control of my life, or whether I was just a lost soul at the mercy of the elements and nature. Does anyone or anything exist in the silence and cloak of invisibility of the night? If I could not see myself or anything else, then what or who actually existed? It was the sense of "I am," and little more. All that I had ever learned, experienced, or thought had lost its meaning and importance as I became the space itself, moving through space, leaving the space untouched. And as I gave myself to the rhythm of gliding through the dark, I found a bliss that came from being nothing at all. For long stretches I felt I was not conscious, as all thought and sensation completely vanished. I knew not what propelled my body onward.

Soon the sun began to peek out from behind the eastern mountains and its light created shadows and forms out of absolute nothingness. At long last I could see the world — including my body — coming into existence, and then in front of me was a little village. Far up ahead was a sign pointing to another railway station. I followed the road for a half hour until I came upon the depot whose copper roof was shining like a beacon.

I purchased a ticket to the next big city, and then sat upon a bench to wait for the very next train to pull up to the landing. Still lost in serenity, I closed my eyes and quickly drifted off to sleep, hoping to recapture the richness of my experience of the night. But I slept only for fifteen minutes or so, because I was awakened by a man kicking my feet and telling me that I was sleeping on his bench. Dazed and with a dry mouth, I looked up at him, and thought he must be joking. I played along, asking how this particular bench could belong to him. But he was serious, and he told me that if I did not move out of his way I would be sorry. I looked at his hands, and his fingers were forming fists. I sprang to my feet and backed away to put a safe measure of space between us. My heart began beating faster, and I did not know what to expect.

"Are you crazy?" I fearfully asked.

The man sneered at me, then ordered me to leave at once. He cursed at me in a loud voice, making others stare at us as they hurried by, too afraid to get involved. I tried to stand my ground as he was rabidly painting me as a criminal. I was a mixture of fear and shock, and I didn't know what to do.

I mustered up some false bravado and told the man, "If you think you can push me around, you'll find out what it's like to be laying on the ground staring up at the clouds. I'm not afraid of you."

But I was afraid. I hardly believed my own words. I was shaking and worried. I was embarrassed by how he was treating me in public, with no good reason. My utterances seemed so empty, absurd and juvenile to me. I did not want to fight, but I did not back down in favor of my own stubborn ego. I stared at his gnarled expression, and the whole scene was quite surreal. I had done nothing at all to provoke this man, and, worse, the peace of the long evening and beautiful sunrise had been shattered by yet another display of human insanity.

The man took a step closer to me, folded his arms over his broad chest, and jutted out his chin. Suddenly his wife and two little daughters came rushing around the corner. His wife asked him what he was doing. She looked at me, then back at her husband, trying to figure out what was happening. Then she grabbed him by the arm and told him that the rest of the family was looking all over for him. She tugged him away, saying that they had found a place to sit on the other side of the station. Then they disappeared into a crowd of people spilling out of a train and onto the platform.

It took nearly a half an hour before I felt my body return to normal. My mind was numb — more confused than angry. Over and over I tried to think of what I may have done to cause such a stupid and outrageous confrontation. Pacing back and forth along the length of the platform, and vigilantly looking out for crazy people, I wondered why people were so full of anger, apparently for no reason most of the time. A knot had formed in my stomach and I was feeling more and more sick to the core. I was sad enough to cry, but too guarded to do so.

When the next train finally arrived, I was glad to be leaving the station and going on my way. One of the first to board, I stumbled through the cars looking for a place to sit. On the way, I happened upon seven robed monks who were enjoying a lively conversation. With great reservations I interrupted them and asked if they had ever heard of the guru whom I sought. They smiled at me then discussed the name amongst themselves before offering me an answer: No, sorry.

With friendly faces they invited me to sit with them, but I thankfully declined and then continued on my way. I found a seat all to myself and settled in by the window. A moment later, a couple of weary middle-aged travelers took a seat across from me, crossed their arms over their chests, and closed their eyes.

I was preparing to stretch out so I could try to resume my nap when a middle-aged woman asked me if she could sit beside me. Just my luck, I thought. I had hoped to have a bench for myself, but now I had to share my space and try to sleep in an upright position. I scooted over and tucked my rucksack between my body and the wall of the train. The lady thanked me and sat down without a fuss. As she was getting settled, I looked up at her and noticed that she had a kind face. She wore a cheerful dress of gold, turquoise and red, and a series of sparkling bangles on her wrists. Her jet black hair was pulled back to reveal a stunning face of pronounced cheekbones and the beauty of youth, though she had to be at least the age of my own mother. But unlike my mother, this woman who seemed to radiate warmth and light, was perfectly content to mind her own business. I turned back to stare out the window, prepared to be bored for the rest of the day by a bleak and endless countryside of dried weeds, farmers, poor little villages, and gray-brown hills.

When the train finally pulled away from the station, I breathed a sigh of relief. I gazed down at my feet, and for the first time noticed the condition of my shoes. I lifted up my foot and discovered that my sole was worn out.

From time to time, out of the corner of my eye I glanced at the lady sitting contently beside me. There was something quite attractive about her — not in any romantic way, but something somehow magnetic or alluring. She had a placid expression and kept to herself as her attention was absorbed in a rather thick book. When she caught me looking at her, she smiled and offered me some food that she had tucked away in her satchel. I refused at first, but she insisted. I would have declined again, but there was no hiding the sound of my growling stomach. I accepted gratefully, and it seemed to bring her joy to watch me eat.

I cannot express the degree to which there was something so inviting and different about this woman's countenance. Though I had never been one for idle discussion or making introductions, I thought of asking her if she had ever heard of the sage whose name I had kept in the fore of my mind for so long. But then I decided not to mention it when I saw that her eyes were slowly closing in response to the monotonous rhythm of the train thumping over the tracks. I was momentarily disappointed not to speak with her. She tucked her book inside her satchel and prepared for a nap. With nothing special to look at through the windows, I too became overtaken by drowsiness. The rocking of the train over the tracks, like a drum beating outside and inside my head, lured me to sleep. Seconds later, I could hear myself snoring and wondered who was making such a sound. Then, despite the persistent rattling and jerking of the train, all went silent and I fell into a deep sleep, dead to the world and unaware of anything at all.

Upon waking, perhaps two hours later, I could not at first make out what my eyes were seeing or where I had found such a soft pillow. When my mind came back into focus, I realized I was staring at the knees and feet of the two passengers across from me, and that the inviting cushion beneath my head was actually the lap of the woman beside me. Deeply embarrassed, I bolted upright, vigorously rubbed my face, and began to apologize for my behavior, but the kind woman smiled and told me that she hoped I had enjoyed my rest. Stuttering past my self-consciousness, I thanked her for her graciousness. A broad smile lifted her cheeks, and then she let out a little laugh. I now felt inclined to talk with her, but she was the first to speak.

The lady asked me where I was headed, and I told her I did not know.

"You don't know where you are going?" she asked sweetly, as if to a little child.

"Well, I do, but I don't," I said.

Next she asked about my family, and I gave her a few details about my upbringing and departure before telling her that I had left everyone I knew behind to wander the countryside.

"Your mother must be heartbroken," she said. "You left without a word or warning? I can't imagine how she feels."

I was suddenly filled with guilt. I lied and said that my mother wished me well on my journey, and that we would meet again before the next rainy season. I am not sure if she believed me.

Fearing that our conversation might die out, I asked the lady where she was going.

She said, "I am returning home. I had a wonderful pilgrimage to see my guru. I go at least once a year, sometimes twice, and it's been ten years now. When you have the right guru, you can be most uplifted and inspired."

Immediately I felt myself pull away. I crossed my arms over my chest.

"It is not my intent to insult you," I said confidently, "but my experience with religion has never been a good one, and all gurus are phonies, frankly speaking. No offense, really, but it's just that they are looking for a free ride from people who support them with full conviction that they are saving their own souls. Anyhow, that's my impression."

I surprised myself with my rude honesty and then suddenly apologized, fearing I had hurt the kind lady's feelings. I studied her expressions, and it was obvious that my strong opinions did not seem to disturb her in the least. In fact, what I had said made her smile, and a motherly sense of love and warmth flowed from her and into me. She said nothing in defense of her guru, and made no excuses for her feelings.

"We all do what the moment brings," she told me, "but no one can just hand you any answers, because all of your problems are for you to figure out for yourself. You will find out, if you are so inclined, that you are not your problems."

I nodded in agreement, but did not truly grasp what she was saying.

"What is it that you are in search of?" she asked.

"I don't know," I said. "Answers. Maybe I am looking for answers. Have you ever just wanted to know the Truth? Not in a mystical or religious sense, but just the Truth. That is all I want. I'm not looking to be a follower or to be given some silly answers to make me feel better. I am sick and tired of that. And I'm tired of life. It makes no sense to me. Does it make sense to you?"

I believe this is the first time I had ever stated my feelings in such a way. Perhaps this is because until that moment I never had anyone to whom I could speak about such things.

"Hmm," said the kind woman. "There is so much suffering, is there not? Also, there is suffering about the suffering itself."

"You just described me. I suffer over the suffering. It's all so senseless, but hardly anyone cares to make a change for the better, don't you think?"

Then it occurred to me that, because she seemed to be genuine and interested in otherworldly teachings, I should ask if she had ever heard of this sage whose name I had long carried with me. So I said I was going to meet a special teacher. She chuckled.

"Why are you laughing?" I asked.

"Because not a moment ago you were telling me how all gurus are phonies, but now you are asking about this one sage. It sounds like you cannot help yourself from going down this road."

"Help myself from what?" I asked.

"From yourself," she said. "You cannot control your passion to know about yourself."

"I don't want to know about myself," I said, "I want to know why this world is so full of terrible people, and why it makes no sense. I want to know the Truth, but perhaps I have lost all hope by now."

"Such a search begins with yourself, don't you think?" she said softly. Then she asked me the name of this guru whom I had traveled so far to find.

When I told her, she placed her hands together and laughed some more as if she were witnessing a great cosmic joke. She said that it was this same sage who had been her guru for many years.

"I just left the ashram only early this morning," she said through her laughter.

In disbelief, I stared at her for much too long, and she did nothing more than smile back at me. But now there was something very different about her smile. It was not just a conveyance of warmth, but something deeper, borne of an unemotional, weightless contentment. There was no hint of pretense or pride. Her smile was a gift that expected nothing in return. There was true peace in this woman, and it melted my heart. I could not look away and found myself drawn deep inside of her so that the rumble of the train and everything visible began to fade into a whirlpool as the people seated across from us stared at us in confusion over our cryptic exchange of such a long, shameless glance.

Suddenly, I returned to my senses as it dawned on me that I was on the wrong train, going the wrong way! I jumped out of my seat and then stopped to realize that there was nowhere for me to go.

If this kindly woman had just returned from seeing this sage, then I knew I must travel back to where she had just been. She happily gave me travel directions and instructions on which train to take and which roads would lead me to this sage whose name had rekindled something within me. She also offered me money, but I declined, telling her I had earned enough to carry me for quite a long time before running out. Regardless, she pushed a wad of money into my hand and closed my fingers around it. I stared at my fist and how it was holding a gift of love from a complete stranger. For this reason only, I could not refuse it.

The next morning, in a dense fog just as the sun began to rise, my new friend bade me farewell, and then I waited six more hours for the next train to come so that I could head back in the direction from which I had just come.

Following another long day in a crowded train, I finally arrived in a small village about an hour's walk from the station. The sun was relentless and baked my head and shoulders as I trudged along a wide and heavily traveled road that began to narrow into a single lane. A great deal of traffic flowed in each direction — carts, groups of people, merchants, animals, small taxis, and farmers shared the tight little road. People were bumping into me, and wagons threatened to run me over, but I remained unperturbed. Thoughts of the lovely lady had filled my head so that all I felt was gratitude and a hope that I had forgotten existed. I could not get her out of my mind.

Large blossoming neem trees created a network of canopies along the highway, yet the heat hardly abated under their shade. The traffic thinned out after passing a fork in the road, and presently I was walking by myself for a long stretch. Up ahead there was a boy in an ox-drawn cart parked in the shade of a tree, just off the side of the path. He was peacefully eating a juicy mango as the animal lazily grazed on tufts of tall grass. I asked the boy if he had heard of the sage whom I sought, and he smiled through wet, red lips then wiped his face with the back of his hand.

Pointing with his mango, he said, "Everybody knows! You are close! Don't give up, my boy!" and, being half my age, he laughed at his own silliness. Offering me a generous slice of his fruit, he said that I should keep walking ahead, perhaps for twenty minutes or so, and I would eventually find what I was looking for. "There's a wooden signpost," he said. "You'll see it — if you can read, that is."

He laughed at his little quip, and I thanked him, then continued on my walk. Around the bend the road began to rise in front of me. The grade became steeper and the few people ahead of me were struggling to climb higher and higher toward the foothills of a lone mountain that I had not even noticed until this point. As I marched onward, I overtook those who were elderly and apparently not conditioned to this sort of physical exertion. My breathing grew audible, partly because of the continually elevating path, and partly due to a sense of anticipation. Then, as the boy on the cart had promised, I spotted the little sign pointing to a well-worn trail lined by a stand of palm trees leading to a very small gate.

I stopped to catch my breath before making my way onto the new trail that was a confluence of several bigger roads coming from several directions. The foot traffic had picked up again so that I was presently in the company of others who were coming and going from the ashram up ahead. As I rounded yet another corner I could see that I was traversing a mountain road, and not far off was a magnificent lake gleaming brightly from the powerful midday sun. It was only two minutes later that I at last found myself completely shaded by large trees and soft-spoken people. Just in front of me was an iron gate bordered by two stone pillars manned by a couple of thin and shirtless custodians who graciously bade me to enter. Suddenly my feet became glued to the ground and I could not take another step. A paralyzing fear came over me. I tried to suck air into my lungs, but I was short of breath. I turned my back to the two ushers and clutched my chest, which was painfully tight. I took a seat at the edge of the trail, thinking that I actually might die right there and then, a few paces from a long-held dream.

After a few minutes of trying to calm my mind, I was able to stand. I put my hands on my hips and just stared ahead at that weathered gate while trying to control a strange vibration that had overtaken my body. My heartbeat was softly pounding in my head, and I backed away from the gate until I bumped into a group of pilgrims coming up from behind me. I was swept along with them, and the last one in their group grabbed me around the waist to steady me. He warmly looked into my eyes and encouraged me to walk along with his friends. Numbly, I shook my head in agreement, gathered my courage, and stumbled onward in the stream of strangers.

In less than a minute, after the pilgrims had left me behind with well wishes, I found myself on a wide and manicured yard of carefully trimmed shrubs and flowering plants. The scene was what heaven might have been like. Or perhaps I was just smitten with the prospects of meeting my own destiny.

Laid out before me was a score of small gardens interspersed between large shade trees and handsomely manicured grounds. Several pools of water were strategically placed here and there, reflecting the sun like mirrors until an occasional bird drifted down for a splash, or a person sidled up to the bank to cool off his feet. Further up ahead there was a small, simple house constructed of white brick, and near that was a long rectangular building with a deep, shady colonnade along the entire perimeter. A few other little buildings, gleaming in white, peppered the property. This was a tiny, self-contained village the likes of which I had never dreamt to encounter. Looking over a green valley and golden lake, the place was brimming with peaceful people and an air of goodness that I could not begin to describe. There was not a trace of dilapidation, filth, or human strife. Or had the heat gotten to me so that now I was romanticizing everything I was seeing and hearing?

In an endless flow of traffic, visitors were coming and going, in and out of the buildings, across the lawns, and through the front gate. Most spoke in soft voices so as not to disturb the intense calmness afforded every blade of grass and flower petal. A few laughed softly with their friends. Others stopped in their tracks, closed their eyes, and pointed their faces to the sun. Not that I could explain why, but I seemed to be uplifted by a lightness that pervaded the atmosphere.

I began to wander the grounds, but with a great air of caution, feeling that I was an intruder into someone's privacy. What right did I have to share this grandeur? Who was I to have earned even a moment in heaven where I could rest my soul?

I approached one of the gleaming white structures, which I assumed housed the dining hall, and the aroma of food began to overtake me, causing my stomach to gurgle in response. It had been days since I had eaten a decent meal. Two young women glided out of one of the buildings then stopped to take notice of me. One of them offered me a piece of bread, and I eagerly accepted with a bow. She giggled and offered me more, but despite my hunger I politely refused, not wishing for her to think of me as a beggar.

I milled about until I was deep into the grounds of the ashram. When I reached a clearing beneath a massive tree where a small cluster of visitors sat to escape the full force of the sun, I took a seat on the ground nearby to rest my rubbery legs and to survey the area. Even with so many people roaming around, engaged in muted conversations, all remained unobtrusive, uncrowded, and quiet enough to find solitude. I laid my head down on my rucksack and closed my eyes, and that's when the entirety of my arduous, tortuous journey overtook me. I succumbed to the deep sleep of death, oblivious to the world, myself, or the tiniest thought.

Facing myself

Following my long nap on the wondrous grounds of the ashram, I sat up to stare blankly at the larger of two buildings across the way. I wondered whether all these people, of all types and ages, were also looking for some vestige of truth to explain this otherwise insane existence. And I asked myself who I was, hoping to discover some secret that so many had sought yet never found over the ages. With so many people seeking the Truth, what chance did I hold of being one of so many to possibly find what I yearned to understand. Why would such a crazy pursuit come true for someone such as myself who had barely paid attention to the wisdom teachings, gurus, and the philosophy of sages? I was certain of very little, except the fact that I was unworthy. Now that I had arrived, what was I doing here? What madness would make me think that there was even such a thing as a true sage with something other than mystical nonsense to purvey?

I sat there in a state of ill-ease amidst the greatest serenity I had ever experienced. Confused and overwhelmed, I did not know what to do next. Now that my mind was no longer focused on the struggle of the journey itself, everything had changed. The once obsessive desire to meet this one sage whom I had waited years to find had turned to ambivalence. Where I should have been elated or excited, I was now reluctant and anxious — almost fearful. The questions I had carried with me for so long seemed too trite to ask — that is, if I were given the chance. I reflected upon what I had done with my life, and how ridiculous it seemed that I should have gone on such a long, fruitless fool's errand. While I still wanted to find the ultimate Truth, I was now feeling homesick, weary, skeptical, and defeated. Doubt flooded my mind, and I was preparing myself for the kind of disappointment that had long marked my life.

To avoid falling into a panic and in fear of lapsing into insanity, I had to ask myself what it was that I had really left behind.

"Protection," my mind quickly answered.

"Protection from what?" I probed.

"The unknown," my mind said.

Who knows if this was the right answer? The mind has a way of convincing one of so much nonsense!

I had left all that I had ever known to be a part of me, yet here I was, still alive and existing without any of it. It appeared as though I had brought my body and my mind with me wherever I went. I began to think of the construction of the sentence I had just thought to myself. Who was the "me" and what was the body and the mind? I wondered who it was that had always noticed such things; who had the insight? Who was asking the questions? Was I now delirious from exhaustion and a lack of nourishment? I cradled my head in my hands and stared into the dirt. The old feeling that I was split in two had come to revisit me. There was the "me" who was this mind and body, and there was also this "me" who was watching my own struggles as a person brimming with woes, feelings, trepidations, sadness, hopelessness, faults, and fears.

What kind of irony had I gotten myself into? I had always harbored a distinct distaste for authority, especially religious leaders of all sorts, yet here I was looking for something — someone — I suddenly feared to find. Despite my nearly insane efforts to arrive at this place, now my pride was too swollen to admit that I needed any help, and this made me both sad and angry.

I gazed across the gardens at the small white house and long outparcel, too frozen under the intense midday sun to venture inside. I couldn't bring myself to budge from the little piece of ground I had claimed. I did not want to humble myself before this, yet another, holy man whose followers clung to his feet and hung on his every arrogant utterance. I would not be such a fool, nor would I ever bow down to anyone. From a mile away I could recognize one of these pompous characters in the cloak of a guru. Perhaps, I considered, I would spend another hour or so and then be on my way. And that's when I thought of the kind lady I had met on the train who spoke so highly of this guru. She seemed to have no ulterior motive for saying that she had such good experiences with this guru. She did not try to sell me on anything at all. Why not trust her? On the other hand, my life had proved that nothing ever changed, so why should I expect things to be otherwise? So I had wasted my time with all of this. At least, I thought, I was able to experience life beyond my own little village. I got out and saw the world and tasted struggle and hardships. At least I had made it to this goal relatively unscathed. This had some value, didn't it? Maybe I should have felt pride for my accomplishment, but I did not in the least.

I looked skyward and, despite the strong sun and scarcity of clouds, a light rain began to fall. I did not bother to take cover, as the water refreshed me to the core. A steady drizzle bounced off the ground, plants, trees, and rooftops. Across the lawn, several visitors began to laugh and dance in the shower, spinning around and around with their hands reaching to the heavens. I wondered if they had lost their minds as so many religious followers seem to do when they have deluded themselves into thinking that this world is really a wonderful place to be. What was the line between ecstasy and insanity?

Then the rain gradually stopped, and the greenery was now even greener, and the flowers were more vibrant, and there was a newness that I could not describe. And it was at this very moment when I noticed a small, slender, dark woman in a white robe exit the building with the colonnade. She paused to survey the landscape before walking across the gardens in my direction. I fully shifted my attention from the dizzy dancers as the woman stopped a few feet in front of me. She sat down, crossed her legs, smoothed out her dress, and laid her walking stick in front of her. Then, in a soft and steady voice, she informed me that in a few minutes dinner would be served in the main hall, and that I was welcomed to join the others inside. I smiled politely, wondering who had sent this servant out to see me. Had someone been watching me from one of the buildings? I squinted my eyes and tried to see through the windows across the way.

"I'm really not too hungry," I lied.

In actuality, I did not want to be in the company of a room full of people worshipping some holy man and carrying on conversations centered on blind adoration and hope. Once again, I found myself irritated to think that I had traveled so long to beg a stranger to teach me about the nature of reality. Thoughts began to race in my head about how, if I were ever to meet this holy man that I would give him a piece of my mind. But he would have to approach me first, because I refused to seek him out and humiliate myself by doing so. Now I had made up my mind that this would be a very short stay, and I was not going into one of those buildings to humble myself before some self-serving guru.

I shielded my eyes and tried to gaze up at the bright sky. A breeze picked up and gently animated the woman's white dress, giving her an almost angelic countenance.

"I think I would prefer to sit outside for a while," I told her. And then maybe I'll be on my way."

She did not answer, but instead just sat with me, as we watched people file into the great hall across the way.

When I turned my attention back to the woman, I noticed that her eyes were deep-set, kind and caring, and I imagined she had found some sort of peace — delusionally perhaps — in the presence of the holy man whom so many seemed to adore. To each his own, I thought. I did not bother to ask her if this was the case. She was entirely content to sit quietly with me and soak in the sunshine. As she did so, I studied her face and mannerisms, and I prepared to defend myself should she launch into a sales pitch for her religious views. But such an opportunity never came, as she did not seem to mind the silence, and was content to just relax beside me.

Apparently quite comfortable with her surroundings, I imagined that this lady must have served at this ashram for quite some time. Her features spoke of youth and serenity, yet she was not young in age. Her hands, though gentle and manicured, were calloused from work. Her black hair was streaked with silver strands, and traces of wrinkles slightly accentuated the smooth skin of her face. She was the rich color of chocolate, and her arms were lean but muscular. When she caught me staring at her, a set of perfect teeth shone brightly, and her eyes danced with bliss. She was not reserved at all to return and hold my gaze, and this caused my brain to play tricks on me. I began to superimpose the face of the lady whom I had met on the train onto the face of this woman beside me. I could not tell why she was smiling at me, and I stared at her for much too long, enchanted and unable to turn away. Then she held out her arms to embrace the space that was owned by no one. Instinctively, I leaned closer to her. She stretched out her graceful, long fingers, and lifted her face toward the sun, like a flower attentive to its source of radiance. I glanced upward as well, as if expecting to see an angel drifting overhead. But there was nothing but sky, sun, and white clouds. And then, as if in response to the inclination of this lovely figure beside me, a cool breeze tickled the leaves of all the trees and swept across our faces and bodies.

Eventually, the silence between us became untenable for me, and I picked up my rucksack and told the kind lady that I would be leaving. I was certain there would be words of protest and a flurry of questions as to my reasons for coming in the first place, yet she remained unaffected. Oddly, despite wanting to leave, as if hypnotized, now I could not move, and she sat with me for another long while.

"Very well," she said to break the silence, "perhaps you would like something to take with you. Some food."

"I am really not hungry," I said.

"You have come a very long way, I am sure," she answered in a motherly tone. "You must eat before you go. Where else would you get your strength from?"

I did not know how to answer, and we rose to our feet in unison. She groaned on the way up and I instinctively held her by the arm to help. At that very moment, a young man came running from the main building to where we were standing. The young man bowed deeply and told her that everyone was waiting to eat.

"Then tell them to eat," she replied with a little laugh.

The young fellow seemed confused and anxious. He began to walk away and then stopped and ran back to her. Then he backed away again and stopped. He came back and stuttered, "But, but...I don't... we cannot begin without you, Guru-ma."

"Of course you may. Go on, and tell everyone they must eat," she insisted. "Go on now. Don't be a pest."

She was serious, yet at the same time very lighthearted in her treatment of the young fellow. Unsure of himself, but with no inclination to argue, he bowed again then rocked back on his heels, transfixed..."

I stood there with my mouth agape as my mind worked to make sense of what was going on.

"Go on," the woman repeated with a graceful wave of her hand. "There will be no waiting. If I am not eating, does that mean that no one is hungry? Please, tell them to eat, and I will be along in due time."

"Of course, Guru-ma," he said.

Then he spun around and reluctantly raced back to the main house. Completely confused, I stared at the woman. My mind reeled. I placed my fingers over my lips. How presumptuous I had been!

"You?" I asked. "You are the one?"

She stifled a laugh, lacing her delicate fingers together and enjoying the revelation that had occurred to me.

It was *her* name I had kept with me at all times. This was the guru I had traveled so far to find? Surely, a joke of the gods had been played upon me. Since first hearing her name, I wrongly assumed that it was a man's name, and never gave it any other thought that the same name could have been fit for either genders. And even in person, I would never have guessed that this unassuming lady could have been the guru whose poorly mocked-up image I had kept so dear to me. But here she was, standing before me in a simple robe draped unceremoniously over a small, lean and taut figure. So strong and defined were her arm and neck muscles, and so deeply tanned was her complexion that I wrongly assumed that such features were those of a servant who had known nothing but hard labor her whole life.

"You have made an image of me." she said, suddenly appearing to be a guru.

"I am sorry," I said, bowing.

"Aren't expectations amusing?"

"I thought you were a servant..."

"*Ha!*" she chuckled, "but I am a servant! Who is not a servant? Is this not so?"

She placed her hand on my shoulder and continued to laugh. Still confused and embarrassed, I did not laugh along with her, and my thoughts were coming fast as my mind tried to adjust to this new way of thinking about her. And then all thoughts stopped and I stood in stunned silence, feeling I should bow deeply in the presence of the guru. This I did, but she showed no change in her demeanor, neither acknowledging my respect nor dismissing it.

Time was standing still. I heard her words, but they were muffled and not making it past my ears. I was lost in her eyes, not as if in a trance or anything so mystical. Not at all. But rather, for the first time in so very long I was not on my guard. The fear of being taken advantage of, and of fighting with some pretentious guru was far from my mind. Tears rolled down my cheeks, yet I didn't know I was crying. A sense of tremendous relief overtook me, and I crumbled to the ground, unable to see anything but her dusty feet. I resisted the urge to take hold of the hem of her robe as I hid my face in my hands, trying desperately to find my equilibrium.

To this lovely, warm woman before me, time had no meaning at all. Despite that a hundred people were anxiously awaiting her entrance into the dining hall, peering out from behind the windows and alongside the columns across the way, she was fully present with me, in no need to go anywhere or be with anyone else.

I stared up at her, spoke past the lump in my throat, and hoarsely said, "I am keeping you from your duties, or obligations, or whatever it is you must do. "

"There is nothing that I am doing," she said.

She placed her hand on my shoulder to steady herself as she sat down beside me. At the same time, the young man returned from the dining hall bearing three plates of food. He served Guru-ma and me, bowed, and then sat himself down a good twenty feet away so as not to be intrusive. The guru waited for me to eat the first bite before she would taste her own food. We did not speak as we ate, and she watched me as a mother would watch her son, joyful that he is feeding his body what it needs. After we had finished, we sat without speaking until I was moved to say something.

"I heard about you quite accidentally," I said. "I overheard your name. I was at the beach and there were two old men… Anyway, it was very long ago…and then I set out to find you."

She nodded with interest. "I see."

"I don't know what I am looking for," I said, hearing the sadness in my own voice. "I suppose I once knew, but now everything is cloudy."

I expected her to laugh at me with a knowingness or some sort of arrogant expression, and this faulty, hapless mind of mine prepared to defend itself. Then a thought occurred to me.

"Do you spend time with all your visitors like this? Is this how it begins?" I said while glancing at the hall filled with Guru-ma's devotees.

"I stepped outside for some fresh air and saw you sitting here," she said.

Guru-ma rubbed her chin and looked at me for a moment, and then she raised her eyebrows.

"Everyone is looking for the same thing," she said softly, "but few know what it is or why." She pointed to the dining hall. "That building is alive with people who say they are searching for the Truth…But how many are ready to know it? They like to hear me speak, and they like to be near me. Some like to touch my feet," she said with a soft smile, "but this will never get them any closer. What they say they want, and what they actually want, are different things. Worlds apart."

"Then why do you allow them to stay with you?" I asked.

"They are flowers responding to the first appearance of the morning sun. Who am I to get in their way? I am no one. It's all quite fine." She paused, then said, "But why are we talking about the others? This is right now about you, isn't it?"

"Yes, about me," I said, finding it difficult to speak about myself.

"What is it that you want? What are you looking for?"

"Don't you know?" I cleverly retorted.

She laughed and said, "I can't read your mind, can I?"

"No?" I asked.

"Of course not," she said.

This surprised me for some reason.

"I thought that's what you do."

I regretted my insolence, but she was unmoved.

We sat for another minute or two before I blurted out, "I only want to know the Truth. I did not come here to worship or be a part of some cult. I do not know who I am, and life does not make any sense to me. It never has. Is it too much to ask — to simply want to get to the bottom of it all, to find out the Truth? I was hoping you could give me the answer, or transfer it to me in some way. I don't know..."

"Let's begin with a simple declaration, if you don't mind," she said. "Whatever you bring with you, in the mind, is all from what you have been told throughout your life. Nothing is original, isn't it so? You have ideas about things. I cannot help you with these ideas, because ideas are ideas, and they never stop coming. To know what you are, you must drop the ideas — the story of who you are and what you think — because they are useless and fleeting. What you want to find is sitting here already, behind all these thoughts. Also, drop your ideas about me, because they are misleading and only get in your way. I am nobody, nothing. Look at the thoughts; do not deny a single one of them. Find out where they come from. Ask yourself the question, 'Who am I?' Find the source of this 'I' and you will know yourself as you truly are."

Leaning heavily on me, she stood up with a little grunt and brushed off her robe so that tiny particles of lint caught the light of day and came drifting down to earth like gold dust.

I nervously said, "I do not wish to be offensive, but how can I trust anything you say?"

She became very serious, and answered, "What good is trust? What does it do for you? This is not about trusting me or anyone else, and it is not about words."

She began to slowly walk away.

"Then why should I listen to you?" I called out.

"No one is making you do anything," she said with kindness.

She slowly continued walking toward the dining hall as her young devotee followed along…

I stood up and called out, "Then what good are you to anyone?"

As I uttered these words of challenge, I immediately recalled my encounter with the priest who had turned his back on me in arrogance and made it a point to belittle me. I was brash, but for good reason. I would not stand to be invalidated by anyone ever again.

Guru-ma turned around, still emanating nothing but sweetness and serenity. She returned to me and took my hands in hers…

"I am not good for most people, it's true," she said softly. "But this is neither my fault nor theirs. All I can do is say something, and then you can see if it is true. This is ultimately your work. Look around…"

I soaked in the scenery — sunlit trees of chattering leaves, bees flitting from flower to flower, a gurgling fountain in the distance, puddles of glistening water pooled in large leaves, and the whole network of beauty comprising the colorful grounds. An elderly man came wandering through the garden with the use of a walking stick, and a lazy cow stood along a small fence, grazing without a care in the world. All was an orchestration of nature, including a handful of people standing on the porch of the long building staring in our direction in anticipation of their teacher's graceful return.

"There is nothing certain in anything you see. These are objects for you. Expressions come and go in your world. Isn't it so? You must be without the objects so that what you see is yourself, and that's all that can be done to know anything of what you call the Truth. I cannot tell you anything that is true, nor can I transfer something to you other than an idea to lead you to yourself. What you do with this idea is completely up to you, isn't it?"

Now there seemed nothing more for me to say, and the guru humbly bowed to me. She repeated that I should keep my mind on the question "Who am I?" and then she walked off with her aide scurrying behind her.

Guru-ma had left me with my mind reeling. I suddenly needed to think everything over, so I headed out far from everyone, and climbed up a steep hill overlooking the ashram and gardens. I felt numb and mindless and I needed to find my bearings. I pondered how it was that suddenly I seemed to know nothing at all.

Regarding what had long cluttered my mind, I asked myself what I actually could know, and how I had come to know it. Which ideas were mine, and which of these did I cling to, and why? How does anyone know anything at all, I wondered. All of these questions, and a hundred more, were posed about a self that seemed not to be entirely me.

The guru's question seemed altogether apropos, and I asked it aloud: "Who am I?"

Days later, in a small room overlooking a courtyard — a place that was to become home to me – I listened carefully as Guru-ma told one of her devotees that each mind is no more than an accretion of thoughts. I thought about this for the rest of the day, then the day after that, and for a very long time. I observed this in myself and found it to be true; the content of the little self — the "I" — is thoughts. But these were not just any thoughts. Instead, they were thoughts about me, my feelings, my fears and desires, and my sense of being a person trying to navigate through this difficult and confusing existence.

With the mind being a collection of thoughts, I questioned what made me hold on to one thought over another one. Why was my mind filled with certain thoughts, while other people seemed to have their own particular thoughts? I asked myself whether anything that I knew was actually earned by way of personal observation, and I reflected on how much we take for granted as fact, yet we call such beliefs "knowledge."

I had to admit to myself that I hardly knew anything at all that had originated with me. But isn't this true of nearly everyone? My opinions and views about the world had never been my own; they belonged to a collection that I shared with all others. Ideas and closely held values had been foisted upon me, ingrained in me, taught to me, and accepted by me without question. I had been conditioned by my upbringing, my father's words, ideas from religious texts and priests, my mother's continuous vapid chatter, words I had read in books, facts my teachers had drummed into my head, experiences that my anger and frustration had brought me, religious teachings, and strong beliefs that were resting on nothing but unchangeable space. I could hear all the voices in my head. I felt myself a fake, for what could I claim to be mine that did not come from someone else? When I asked myself at that moment: "Who am I?" I had no answer once I had discounted all that I had come to call knowledge, opinions, memories, and ideas.

As I observed scores of people coming and going, talking, sharing ideas, praying, and exchanging gestures, I began to see them all as equally conditioned. What were they communicating, except for ideas and memories that were not really their own? I had to ask myself if this was the way of the entirety of humanity. Of course it was. For a flash, I even wondered whether any of us were individuals at all, or whether we were all just borrowing from the same library of ideas and passing them along to one another, painting a new face on them, and recirculating them over and over again as if they were of the utmost importance and had been held so tightly as to shape an image of who we considered ourselves to be.

Who could be proud of any accomplishment if it had not been garnered by one's own personal discovery? Through all this thinking that went on for weeks until my head ached, I came to realize that I was the embodiment of ignorance, unaware of who I was or why I existed. The most pompous among us — proud of their book learning, facts, and scientific and religious teachings — are equally as ignorant.

Again and again I returned to that little question with which Guru-ma had left me: "Who am I?" These three little words amused me, then haunted me, then teased me and provoked me. Who did I consider myself to be? Who realized anything? I needed to separate myself from the tiresome, universal habit of thinking myself to be the self, this sense of an "I" that was some idea about me as a person who was the center of thinking, action, and beingness. But this would take much more than wishing, believing, learning, or assuming. This self was the center of all my suffering, and of this I was now certain.

Without a place to be in the world, I decided to take up residence at the ashram, figuring that perhaps there was yet something I could learn from this particular guru after all. I remained to myself as much as possible, because it was clear that self-discovery, as Guru-ma had first told me, could be nothing other than a solitary path.

Even though I was lost and needed guidance, I could not cleanse myself of a deeply entrenched skepticism about all teachers, priests, and experts, including this guru who seemed far too normal to be a holy woman. I recalled what one of the old men had said on the beach when I had first heard her name — that this guru had such a small following of devotees and was not very important as gurus go. Almost against my will, this memory fortified my skepticism and lack of trust for anyone. In retrospect, my attitude was based on the very thing I was working to rid myself of — taking what was learned second-hand as valid information. Regardless of my self-conflicting attitudes and confusion — or perhaps because of them — I decided to stay with Guru-ma to see where she might lead me.

With each passing week, as I began to let down my resistance, I grew to like my teacher. She had a soft-spoken way about her, but given the circumstances, could be fierce and powerful. Yet her patience for me knew no bounds. She had no inclination or reason to convince anyone of anything, no drive to convey her wisdom or to comment on anyone's state or progress. She did not engage in discussions on politics, topics about equality, how to live a spiritual life, the state of the nation, how to become a better person, how to resolve personal problems, or how to exercise the imagination. She did not entertain anyone's dreams or talk about life experiences; nor did she care to discuss a person's "amazing spiritual experiences." Instead, her message remained simple and forever connected to the same message — Find out who you are by discovering the nature of the I-thought.

"The instant you say, 'I am,'" Guru-ma told me, "something transformative has taken place...Leave it at that; it is unnecessary to add an object onto the end of these two little words. Leave it at 'I am,' and meditate on this."

Although I was never asked to do so, I donated most of my remaining savings to the ashram as fair exchange for my room and meals. After doing so, I sent a letter to my parents telling them of my travels and new residence. I apologized for any hurt that I had caused, and along with the note, I repaid them twice the money I had taken from them on the day I had walked away from my life with them. Money held very little value to me now, as I had become fully focused on finding the Truth about life and the source of all suffering — my suffering and the suffering of everyone who had ever lived.

I reflected on my former life with my family in our little village, and contemplated my father's anger, my mother's vanity, my brother's self-centeredness, and my own bottomless frustration that led to a lifetime of tirades, restlessness, lack of focus, fear, and severe sadness. Was I made of all these things as well, being that this was my world, my experience? In turning my meditations onto myself, I was to observe all of what this sense of "I" seemed to be. For a lifetime I had seen the faults in others, how they had hurt me, and how I had reacted. But now it was time to shine the light on this muddled sense of self that appeared to hold me in chains. Perhaps, I hoped, I would at long last find the cure to the suffering I had wrought, witnessed, and experienced.

You are not just the body — the first pillar

In the span of my tenure at the ashram, I had attended a great number of Guru-ma's talks, and these served to generate even more questions in me. At times I struggled to understand what she was saying, with much of it seeming to be obscured by paradoxes and concepts that were senseless to the logical mind. It became apparent that language failed to communicate much at all, and at best it only provided fodder for the ego mind.

Regardless of anything that I had heard, I continued to explore the question "Who am I?" so that it became a constant mantra all my waking hours. For a long while, the question seemed to have no meaning in the same way as when you repeat a word over and over and it begins to sound foreign. And then the question became quite personal, probing me to find out if I could find an identity that I could call "I." Who, I wondered, was even asking this question?

With persistent observation, I found that I had no way of identifying myself with anything at all. I asked myself whether this "I" — this being whom I called "me" — was connected to a country, village, relatives, my role as a son, or even a gender. But it was not. I inquired as to whether this "I" could be this body with which I had so long lived, tried to care for, neglected, celebrated, hated, protected, and depended upon. But, due to its ever-changing nature, it became clear to me that this "I" was not the body. I even considered whether the five senses that allowed me to feel, taste, see, hear, and smell were connected to the true essence of who I was. They were not.

Guru-ma had said that when enough time and effort is placed on searching for the "I," and the ultimate Truth is found, an amazing revelation takes place.

Eventually I was to discover for myself what my guru had told me: "You are not just the body. The identification and attachment with the physical body, including the brain, and all that the body is said to be, obscures your true nature." She said, "The body carries on a great many functions, heartbeat, digestion, breathing. It houses the brain and is the recipient of all that the senses experience. It allows awareness to experience the world. But we are not aware of most of what goes on with regard to the body's activities. Isn't it so?"

I thought about this and asked her, "But this is my body, is it not? I know it to be mine. I feel it and I see the world through it."

Guru-ma answered, "You say the body is yours, but you are not managing it at all. Trillions of cells are interacting in the body, and they will continue to replicate, function, move, transform, fight, and die without a 'you' to ever be aware of this happening. The lungs breathe in and out without 'you' having to make this occur. There are wars being fought to the death as cells are ousted by other cells that police the body in order to perpetuate its life and health. All during your waking and sleeping hours the heart pumps blood throughout all the vessels of the body, and the brain is always engaged in electrical activity and signal-sending. These functions never cease throughout the life of the body, but 'you' remain ignorant and uninvolved in these goings-on regarding the activities of the vital organs, cells, tissues, and nerves. Is it your choice to age, to become sick, or to become tired?"

"Yes," I agreed, "all these functions take place. But they are *my* functions, are they not?"

"Who are you?" she asked. "Think about this. Who takes credit for all these activities of the body? The self — that which calls itself 'I' — has nothing to do with the existence or perpetuation of any of the body's myriad activities or responsibilities. Nor does it give life to the body or direct its actions from birth to development to aging to death. Yet the self wants to take credit for the body. It puts itself at the center and wants to claim that it has caused you to be good-looking, tall, short, intellectual, athletic, pink, brown, or yellow. The self also wants to take credit for a certain role in the family such as son, daughter, mother, father, brother, or grandparent. But ask yourself: What does the self have to do with physical traits, abilities, extroversion, introversion, sexual preference, gender, deformity, handsomeness, or height?"

Guru-ma told me that the mind states, "I am," then what follows is an identifying word that truly has nothing at all to do with the core of who one is: I am Indian. I am Chinese. I am British. I am African. Are any of these actually inherent to your true nature? What is your true nature? Unless you turn your thoughts inward in attentive observation to uncover this Truth, then you will never realize that the self and the body have nothing to do with it.

"The identities of the self are borne of mental conditioning, such as identifying with a certain political party, tribe, fraternity or sorority, religious belief or atheism, or sports team. The self believes itself to be a follower, an independent, a rebel, a loyalist, a devotee, a warrior, a pacifist, or a leader. It builds a strong identity with the characteristics and features of the body: I am tall, I am big-boned, my feet are small, I am handsome or ugly. I have a strong constitution. I am dark skinned. I am fair skinned. I am skinny. The self identifies strongly with one's occupation such as scientist, teacher, porter, farmer, priest, doctor, or lawyer. Can you truly be any of these things? Only an honest inquiry shall bear the true answer. Otherwise you are merely laying thought on top of thought. What's needed is a lightbulb of recognition to shine on the truth."

One evening, Guru-ma carried a cup of tea onto the grounds and sat on a bench beneath a leafy tree. It was a cool night with a gentle breeze, and she gazed up at the stars while a small audience began to form at her feet. I sat down, away from the crowd but close enough to hear her conversation with a devotee who wanted to know how her mind came to be so problematic.

"The mind is a terrible thing," the devotee said.

"No," Guru-ma answered. "The mind is not this nor that. The mind is an instrument that helps you find your way through this world. It pays attention and remembers what takes place. It knows how to speak and how to use things. It is quite practical, isn't it so?"

"But the Buddha has said that it is the instrument of suffering."

"Is this what you know, or are you offering yourself the teachings of another? What is it that you can say that you know for yourself?"

"It seems to me that the Buddha was right. The mind is always causing suffering."

"Not the mind," Guru-ma answered. "How did the suffering come to be, other than by way of focusing on, and obsession with, objects, including the ultimate one — the body? Do not confuse the instrument called the mind with the conditioned thoughts that it clings to. It is this conditioned mind — the self — that is obsessed with the transient, and it identifies with the objects taken in by the senses."

"Objects?" asked the devotee.

"By objects, we are speaking of material things and ideas. The self, as the conditioned mind, presents a false picture of who you actually are, isn't it so? There is no characteristic, identity, or trait that is permanent; each one fades and then disappears with time. When you are young you may be short, but when you are older you may be tall. You may be weak as a youth but strong by age thirty. You may be sickly today and healthy tomorrow. Such attributes come and go, yet there is a 'you' that remains through all the apparent changes, independent of the body. Who is this 'you'?"

As I listened to Guru-ma speak, I thought to myself: "These are words of wisdom, no doubt, but how can they be known as truth?" And, as if hearing my thoughts, she told the devotee, "The answer is realized through inquiry into one's own nature. Observation makes this known. Why would you choose to identify with the body? You are used to doing so, owing to a lifetime of practice. You have been told since birth to claim 'this is my body,' and to identify with it and everything related to it. Does water claim that it is the cup in which it is contained? Does the cup claim that it is the space in which it resides?"

I began to think about this idea of conditioning and how early it begins in one's life. As a baby, your mother tells you this is your nose, this is your mouth, this is your name, this is your father, this is your home, this is your brother, these are your toys. When you grow a little older you are told that this is your religion, this is your school, and this is your nationality. You are conditioned to be proud of all of these because they are said to be a part of you — they define you to the core. But what does any of this actually mean? Does the body know that it is a girl or a boy? Does it know that it is a Muslim, Hindu, Jew, Sikh, or Christian? Does the body know it is a fan of a sports team? Does the body teach you to hate a foreigner? The self makes these petty differentiations, not the body.

In a subsequent meeting, Guru-ma told me, "Yours is clearly no longer the same body that you knew in childhood. It has changed in countless ways, yet you continue to claim it to be you; you persist in identifying with it. Which body is the real you? The one in the womb? The one that was an infant? That of the two-year-old? The twenty-year-old? The one you knew from a past life? You as a decrepit old man? Even the scientists tell us that this week's body has none of the same atoms in common with last week's body, which means that there is a completely different body whom you call 'I' each and every week. By the end of your life, which one of the thousands are you? How can you be associated with something so changing and fragile, and yet still be able to say, 'This is who I am?'

"Having emanated from consciousness — the great stream flowing out of the Absolute wholeness of eternity — that has created the body, you cannot be the body. Since consciousness exists prior to thoughts, you are none of the thoughts that you notice or cling to. Arising out of consciousness are the thoughts that comprise the mind, so you cannot be the mind either. You must have been here prior to the formation of the body. One who says, 'I am' is a more consistent existence than the body. But this particular 'I' that exists independent of the body is not the ego-you; it is not the conditioned self. Even the words 'you' or 'I' are inadequate and false. All that can be known is an existence in consciousness. The body, mind, and all expressions arise out of consciousness. And beyond this, behind it, beneath it, encompassing it, comprising it, is the Absolute that is neither change nor form. Ultimately, this is who you are, and in this stateless state there is no 'who' at all. You need not confuse who you are with fleeting expressions, bodies, traits, activities, and experiences."

Guru-ma's words confused and intrigued me, leading me into a deeper search of my own sense of beingness. I wondered at first why one does not identify with the Absolute state that "is" even prior to consciousness if indeed one is not the self or the body. Why are we so distracted from the Absolute as that which we truly are? Only with enough time would it become obvious to me that, owing to habit, we do not know our true nature. We have been misled by others who had been misled by those who came before them. The misinformation is like a virus, passed along to us in a strong chain of ignorance. Each person erroneously informs the next generation that he/she is the body. Then, events and thoughts adhere to this false identification with mind and body, and they build upon it. The belief that arises is difficult to dismiss, because it is much like hypnosis or amnesia. Only with an honest look at the characteristics claimed to be oneself, and with the deepest inquiry into the origin of the ego-self, without settling for an easy answer, will the mind question its own existence. It will ask, "Who am I?" or "What is at the very core of existence?" With great attention upon this inquiry, the hypnosis begins to wear off.

Anyone can see, with enough inquiry into the nature of the self, that the body comes into form, constantly changes, and then eventually runs its course until it ceases to function.

"Look around you," Guru-ma said, "— there are babies, children, teens, young adults, middle-aged parents, and the elderly. There is an apparent constant change of mind and body. All the while, existence remains as existence. But even behind this is that which remains nameless, present, and indescribable. It is there all along, and does not change — an endless, uncancellable space over which all that we call reality is superimposed.

"You are concerned with this body because it serves only to perpetuate and support the ego 'you' who identifies as it," Guru-ma said. "The self, a belief, persistently reminds itself and others that it is associated with the body. But where is this self that spreads such misinformation? Look for it and discover the crux of your problem.

"The body has never claimed that it is permanent or in fear of loss and injury. Only the self has made such claims. Obviously, the body is impermanent, yet the self is in denial and does not want to admit of the body's temporal reality. It does everything in its power to extend the life of the body, and it fears illness, aging, injury, inconvenience, pain, and death, despite that all of these are inevitable, unavoidable."

I wrestled with Guru-ma's words, which were all new to me. I pondered whether it is logical to ever say, "I am the body, or I am so-and-so." To claim "I am the body" is similar to saying "I am afraid, or "I am sad," or "I am hungry," or "I am tired." It is pairing the "I am" of conscious awareness with an ephemeral state or object. She or he who says, "I am saddled with this body, I am stuck with it," is firstly speaking from an "I" that is the ego mind, the self that has been conditioned by ideas. The consciousness that created the body would not say that it is the body. How could it, when it obviously precedes the body and the mind? So what are you?

There is a permanence to the Absolute that resides even behind existence — that is, movement, creation, action, birth, and death. This Absolute is like the space that fills a cup. The cup may shatter and be swept away, but the space remains unchanged, unmoved. When the body dies, it does not take the Absolute along with it. It is this remaining absoluteness that is so easily overlooked. It is always here, but the attention is ignorantly placed upon the body instead.

No thoughts are your own
– the second pillar

On occasion, the question as to who I was — who I thought I was — haunted me, for I could find no answer. I spent many sleepless nights tossing and turning as my mind mulled over questions of my own existence and my relationship to this confusing and complicated world. Too many times I approached my guru to say that I was suffering over this most egregious riddle, yet her answer was never satisfactory for the self. She would say, "Find out who it is that suffers," and then she would dismiss me.

I questioned whether an "I" existed at all. If not, what was it that existed, for I certainly still, even without fully identifying with the body, knew that I existed. This began to sound like a maze of thoughts. The "I" who knew that there was existence was not the "I" who was the self, but there was no other word than "I" that could be used to represent the one inquiring into this existence.

There is an "I" that is present always, with or without thinking of the "I" or anything else for that matter. If I could not find this egoic, personal sense of "me" — if it really did not exist — then who was doing anything? Who was moving this body about, and who was answering to this name that I had been given? I must admit that it wasn't long before even my name began to seem foreign to me. Was I a "doer" in this life, or just the expression of some greater motion beyond the mind and body that was called consciousness? Eventually I would find out.

Everyone has the sense of "I," leading me to consider whether the world was teeming with deluded people. Could it be that the body is doing the action by some energetic means while the ego "I" merely claims to be the doer? If so, this would mean that people are all under some sort of mass hypnosis, thinking themselves to be something that they are not.

After many more months had elapsed, I began to inquire into the emotions that dwelled within me. Now the question "Who am I?" took on yet another shade of meaning, and I looked deeply at the varied emotions that occupied a large space in my thoughts. I wondered whether emotions, as thoughts, were part of this "I-self." Where did they come from? Why did I seem to hold onto some quite strongly, while other emotions held little sway over me? Why, for instance, had anger taken up such residence within me, while jealousy had hardly played a part in my life? Why were some people envious while others were more prone toward vanity? What did any emotion have to do with the real "me" for whom I searched?

When I had first arrived at the ashram I felt it to be a place of tranquility and introspection, but I slowly came to realize that this was only a matter of perspective and potential. The tranquility was but a matter of potentiality and could easily be supplanted by the mind's preoccupations. With enough time to search for my own sense of beingness, it became obvious that I had brought my suffering with me, from hundreds of miles away, and the freedom that I originally sought was really freedom from this self that I carried around wherever I went.

"Meditate upon your own condition," my guru told me.

"But I cannot quiet my mind and make the thoughts stop," I complained.

"Who has asked you to do such a silly thing?" she answered. "This kind of forcefulness is not a meditation that challenges the 'I-thought.' Meditate. Think, ponder, consider, dive deep within, looking always to see what is there. Look deep within yourself to shed light on all of the contents. Bring no judgment or criticism to this meditation. Just observe. Do that."

I walked away with a mission in mind — to explore the nature of myself, where thoughts were coming from, and whether there was an "I" that was having the thoughts. Through this meditation I observed that thoughts arise spontaneously. This was quite simple to do, as if watching fireflies coming and going across my field of vision. And where did these thoughts come from? Out of a vast stream of potential and movement that we may call consciousness. Consciousness is the factory for thoughts. Thoughts arise without personal control, and I observed this happening, not as the creator of thoughts, but as the watcher of them. If I was truly the doer, then who was making thoughts happen without my permission or control?

The thoughts I agreed with, or felt reinforced my image of myself, others, or the world at large — or the ones that made me feel safe in my image — became attached to my ego-self, reinforcing what thoughts, concepts, and ideas that were already there. So out of a vast reservoir of thoughts, existing in a stream of consciousness, specific thoughts clung to my sense of self, according to my psychological conditioning.

And so I reflected on the anger that I had known nearly my whole life. Could this anger be the reason why I had continually met up with angry people and situations? Was this the reason I became entangled with anger over and over again? And what of other people who had problems with anger — were they realizing their own opportunities to know anger-filled situations based on their tendencies to think one way or another? The apparent fact that consciousness held the potential to present thoughts told me that all thoughts must be universal and are not personal at all. They lie in waiting — in potential — in a stream of consciousness ready to be realized or not, depending on the self's tendencies.

Many spiritual seekers and meditators talk about needing to get rid of the mind, or in the least to quell it. But look what is happening. The mind is only an instrument, but when it is conditioned by thoughts that lead you to believe there is an "I," a self, then it becomes a belief that drapes a veil over consciousness. So it is not the mind that is the cause of suffering, but rather this belief that there is an "I." And with this belief also comes the belief that you are all the things associated with the body's journey through life — your awards, relatives, ideas, memories, possessions, friends, sports team, job title, accomplishments, and so forth. Meditating in silence and concentrating upon the breath alone does not address this facade of a self, nor does it wake you up to the fact that you identify with the body. Trying to be a better person or repeating affirmations may be a peaceful, uplifting experience, but these do nothing to let you become aware of your false identity.

Over and over again I listened to visitors ask Guru-ma whether their thoughts should be sought out and destroyed. She would tell them that such a question comes from conditioning — something they have heard needs to be done. We've all heard how we have to quiet the mind, make it stop, stop the thoughts, turn the mind into a slave instead of a master, and so on. But how wise is this sort of advice when this is not the seat of the issue?

The mind is not bad, errant or troublesome. It allows us to move through this world, interact with others, and see the beauty in all things. It is only when the mind becomes conditioned to identify with the body, ideas, objects, people, memories, information, and so on, that we experience suffering. The practical mind must not be confused with the ego mind — the self. Clearly, without a mind that has memories, there would be no way to find your way home or who your friends are.

By observation it becomes evident that all thoughts arise from the same, one and only consciousness. It is the egoic mind, and not the practical mind, that leads us to identify with the body, creates lasting trauma, judges all events, worries endlessly about the safety of the body, fears losing possessions or social standing, and interprets actions as good or bad. Thoughts are not inherently good or bad; they merely come and go, and only the conditioned mind — that which you call "I" — holds onto them so that they create a belief system that informs you that your existence is tied to objects.

Duality makes knowing possible — the third pillar

A visitor sat at the feet of the guru and stared at her for a long while as if in a daze, with eyes glazed over and an expectation of miracles. Guru-ma glanced down at him and waited patiently. After a long while, he cleared his throat and said that there would be no problems if only people would live their lives in non-duality.

"The non-dual reality," he continued, "is where all happiness may be found, because it is not rife with conflict, squabbles among people, destruction, or difficulties."

When the guru said nothing in response, he waited another minute and then asked her if she would advise him how to live a non-dual life.

"Who is asking such a question?" she answered. "Who could exist in this state that you call non-dual? Anyone can look around and see shapes, sizes, colors, forms, textures, and images that differentiate one thing from another. Where are you getting this idea of non-duality other than from another who is ill-informed and making such suppositions?"

And then Guru-ma turned her attention on her little audience.

"Perhaps you have heard that the ultimate Truth is that there is only a oneness, just a unified reality. Is this, too, another idea? Or do you know it to be so? Find out for yourself instead of repeating ideas from others..."

But the inquisitor was persistent. He said, "I have heard even you say that that there is a oneness — a wholeness — that is the true reality. I would like to know this non-dual state."

"You are sitting before me with a body and mind, is it not so?"

"Of course, Guru-ma."

"The world that the mind knows is not, and can never be, the ultimate reality. The mind fragments the oneness into pieces. To see light, there must be darkness as its contrast; and to know cold there must be the complement of hot. A large animal can only be distinguished from a small one because there is fragmentation by the mind that places all expression into categories and comparisons. Without this fragmentation we would all be walking into walls and forgetting how to speak to one another. Certainly there is a non-dual Absolute, but it cannot be known by the mind. The mind's means of existence, operation, sustenance, and perpetuation is due only to duality, that which separates one thing from another. What you call non-duality is as much of a concept as duality."

"So," asked the devotee, "should we not aspire to this non-dual state?"

"You may aspire to whatever state you would like," answered Guru-ma, "but aspirations take you only so far. If you want to realize non-duality, it will not be by way of the mind, for it precedes mind, body, and consciousness. To aspire is, at some point, a mind exercise. The self is forever searching for new ideas to latch onto. It seizes upon a new way of looking at things and objectivizes it as it does with everything else. Today you may say you want to be enlightened, and tomorrow you want to experience the oneness. The following week it may be that you have heard non-duality is the state that you need to reach. These are all just more ideas to entertain the self, getting you no closer realizing the Truth."

Guru-ma said that the point when you metaphorically step out of the unformed stillness behind all of what the "I" calls reality, a world of duality appears to exist. "Duality means that all exists in comparison to all else — good to bad, tall to short, strong to weak, and me versus you. There is no way to know or learn anything — or to think or communicate or use the senses — without duality. No sound, light, language, or experience could occur without duality. How would this body fare in such an absurd state?"

The Absolute in which everything exists and which is the substratum of all, lies in complete stillness, infinity, and silence. It is non-dual, but the concept of it is dualistic.

Nothing can describe this Absolute, because to describe it would take duality. Such is the paradox of Truth: You ARE the Truth, but you can never know this Truth with the limited mind.

Duality converts everything into subjects and objects. As a concept of the mind, it separates the fabric of totality — the oneness of existence — into fragments. This is advantageous to move through the world of forms and expression — to communicate, travel, use the senses, work, play, create, destroy, and so on. But this is not why we suffer.

"The self believes that fragmentation is the true reality, because it is ignorant of the Absolute and, in this ignorance it can know nothing but a fragmented existence," said Guru-ma. "It is in this fragmentation that the belief of two or more opposing objects — you against the other — is imbued in the self. This separation of the whole is what causes immeasurable suffering."

With enough introspection, it is possible to discover that, in this duality that we commonly call life, or our world, everything you see, know, touch, feel, think, and experience may add to your mental conditioning. This conditioning is compounded and cemented in large part by thoughts that come from memories, teachings, advice, emotions, experiences, impressions, ideas, and so forth. That which remains, when all of these thoughts are gone and there is total attention on the present, is not describable, measurable, or subject to the rules of time or space. It may be called the non-dual state, but even this does not explain what it is, because it is not actually a state, and it cannot be conceptualized and still remain accurate. The mind cannot know the formless, non-dualistic essence, so anything that the mind reports about it is not it.

Guru-ma said that duality allows for conditioning of the mind, all action, and the appearance of thoughts. You would not even be able to say, "I am" unless duality preceded this these two words, because language requires duality. Thought does as well. "Forget this idea of living a non-dual life. It is but another idea that leads you away from that which you seek," she said.

Following Guru-ma's discussion on non-duality, the room fell quiet. The man who had brought up the topic sat in stunned silence as if disappointed that this concept that had so intrigued him had been turned to dust. By the look of his expression, he was not accepting what Guru-ma had said, and instead wanted to pursue this state that he thought would lead to his self-realization. So he gave it one more try.

The man argued, "But if non-duality is the Absolute, then why not aspire to achieve it?"

Guru-ma stared at him for a moment so that his mind might quiet down long enough to listen. She said, "Non-duality is not the Absolute. There is no quality or description for the Absolute. You are already That. There is nothing to achieve or find, for such actions can only be done in movement; and the Absolute is absolute stillness, prior to all movement. Your ideas are fogging your glasses. You are looking all over for the space that you cannot see. You are in the space and inseparable from it, yet you search for it as if it is far away from you. Why do you do this?"

With that, Guru-ma calmly arose and walked out of the hall.

Time and again I had heard people trying to engage Guru-ma in discussions on non-duality, but she treated the topic like any other that has to do with concepts that lead no further to the realization of one's true nature.

I came to realize that those who speculate about non-duality often speak of it as if it were a thing, a place, or a state of being, but this is just one more concept they have accumulated. Non-duality is a phrase that fails to explain anything. It is tossed around without regard for its inherent self-contradiction. To use Guru-ma's expression: "Talk of non-duality is a futile attempt to give the nameless a name." If you are thinking of something, speaking of it, writing about it, or portraying something by any means, whether as art, writing, dance, speech, poetry, or gestures, then it cannot be non-dual. If it is beyond all of these expressions then it cannot be spoken of as either this or that; neither dual or non-dual. People do not live in non-duality as long as they engage in the world of form and as long as they are people. How silly is it to say "I want to talk about non-duality," for it is like saying, "Let's discuss silence."

*To dwell on definitions and concepts is fruitless.
You must let them go and cede to silence.*

Abide in the 'I am,' not the object — the fourth pillar

Guru-ma sat by a large window reading the daily newspaper and sipping tea. A soft breeze swept through the building and ushered away the heat. Finding Guru-ma alone was a rare event, so I decided to sit across from her and ask if I could share my experiences. She put down her newspaper and looked at me.

"Each day living in the ashram I have been occupied with looking into my own nature," I told her. "It seems ironic that of all the things that we know, we know the least about ourselves. I have meditated for hours on end observing the mind. It has taken me a long time, but now I can see how it functions, how it has been conditioned to produce mental tendencies."

In turn, I explained, these mental tendencies seem to unify with thoughts that arise out of the potentiality of consciousness. The attachment to thoughts — especially those that reinforce the belief that a person is his body — seems to be the source of all suffering for everyone.

I told my guru, "It is apparent that I need to free myself from my own mind."

"You are already free," she said. Then she picked up her newspaper and reclined on her couch to bury her face in it.

Unaffected by Guru-ma's apparent disinterest in what I had to say, I continued anyway. I said that I had looked into it, and could see that the self was imprisoning me and causing all my suffering. I was somewhat proud of this discovery, and I had expected her to laud me for it, but instead she peered over her newspaper and asked, "Who is this 'I' who seeks to be free? Who is bothered by the suffering? Who is looking to be unchained and to escape from suffering? Who suffers?" Then she turned the page of her newspaper and returned to her reading.

On a subsequent day, I was sitting by myself in the dining hall when one of the guru's devotees joined me and began to talk about how he could feel the guru's internal energy being transmitted to him, filling him with a sense of realization of the ultimate Truth. I stared at him for a moment and marveled over how much this young man looked like me — my age, height, build, and even similar facial features. He also had a certain intensity to him, seemingly determined to have his ideas accepted and embraced. I mulled over whether I should respond to his statement or remain quiet.

Perhaps a minute passed before I told him that his idea of a guru's transference of energy was nonsense, because such feelings were his own projections. Guru-ma had once told me that no such thing occurs, but this person sitting beside me persisted in arguing his point, and, without pause I began to argue back. After a few minutes or so of this useless and intense bantering, and in a fit of anger, the young man stormed out of the hall in disgust with me. I found myself sitting alone and seething with rage.

I rushed outside in a sweat as if I were starving for air. I found a spot beneath a tree, plopped myself down and pushed my back against its massive trunk. I closed my eyes, hoping to calm down by clearing my thoughts. But it was impossible to find stillness as the angriest sorts of thoughts took complete possession of my mind. I sprang to my feet, and then set off on a long, fast walk, hoping to disperse the rage that had welled up so quickly in my body.

I became determined to observe my anger without feeding into it or judging it, but this was not an easy thing to do. At first I thought of the young man and how stupid he was to believe so strongly in absurd notions. I instantly recalled my one-time companion whom I had met during my journey. I remembered how he had so much wanted me to buy into his cult and sway me to his beliefs. Then I realized that I could have easily reconstituted all sorts of memories of other people who had angered me over my life. But instead of entertaining such anger, I simply placed my attention on observing what was going on with me. I turned my thoughts back to this little self that I called "me." I fought with my mind to push it back to face that one annoying question that had grown nearer to me than my heart: "Who am I?" I asked myself who it was who was filled with so much rage. This was proving to be a most arduous task, to overcome the immediacy and power of the emotion, and to find a way to divorce myself from it long enough to observe it. For a split second I wondered who it was who was witnessing the anger and inquiring into its source.

I sat for another hour or so and observed the nature of anger and my relationship to it, holding onto it as if it were a wild cat struggling to wrest itself free from its tether or turn around and claw me. Yet another hour passed and I was still sitting with this rage, and I continued to look at it until I came to realize that I was the rage itself.

I was the rage. It was inseparable from the "I." I asked the question, "Who am I?" and then I answered, "I am anger." This is what I had to admit in all honesty. There was no difference between myself and the emotion of anger. It was contained within the container called "I."

Even now, as I convey these words, I cannot clearly explain what this means or how it felt, but it was an admission that was shocking, disheartening, and freeing all at once. It was an admission that I had not grown to become anything better than the day I had left home on my journey to find Guru-ma. But this simple realization marked a cornerstone for me.

The longer I had thought about it, the more this acceptance that the ego-I and the rage were the same, a shift in my being came into focus. Both the ego-I and the rage were contained within consciousness itself. The experiencer and the experience were of the same fabric.

Somehow this admission of unity between self and emotion served to dispel a monumental conflict within me. Paradoxically, outside of this little self of the ego, I realized that I was not only the rage, but I was equally not the rage. I was everything and, as everything, there was nothing left to cause a conflict within me. There is a unity to everything, and when there is a unity then there is no division; it takes division to create conflict.

As the result of steady observation, now I had come to know an emptiness in the place of where the rage had been. What more, I wondered, comprised this "I" that could be causing so much suffering? Was I the "I"? For the moment it felt as though I was not.

I discovered that this ego-self that I thought myself to be, was the very anger that it had taken as an object. There was a relationship — a marriage — between the "I" and the object, the emotion. And this marriage was created and perpetuated by the way I tended to think, based on how the self had been conditioned.

All of my life I had been blaming my anger on other people and on situations, making objects out of them as if they were the real causes. The more I sat with this, the more layers peeled away. I knew that the devotee with whom I had argued was only an excuse for my anger — and I was an excuse for his. I had made an image of him, and he had made an image of me. Acting from ego, our actions served only to divide us into individuals, when in fact we are one consciousness.

The anger that I had known was only a concept in search of an object. It stood for something. It was all anger, a universal anger, and the universal anger had no object at all until the conditioned self got hold of it. It simply sat in waiting —in potentiality — for those tendencies that would bring it into existence. It took this self, filled with anger, to know anger and to find anger. The one who is enraged is the very thing over which he is enraged.

When the mind places its attention upon objects then it obviously is not turning inward to know itself. This bit of knowledge kept me vigilant so that I was determined to focus on this "I" instead of external objects as the source of all conflict and suffering.

When I next sat in on one of my guru's morning discussions, I asked a simple question and then sat down to listen. It wasn't even really a question. I wanted a confirmation of my own realization. I asked Guru-ma to talk about the self's relationship to objects, and she responded with one simple sentence: "Abide in the 'I am,' not the objects."

Then she explained:

If you are constantly fixated upon an object, then you are always keeping your attention on the things of the self — the assumed individual — that you believe yourself to be.

Consider the structure of basic grammar, and how a sentence works when you communicate. There is a subject, a verb, and an object. The self thinks, "I am depressed about my relationship." In this sentence, "I" is the subject, "am" is the verb, and "relationship" is the object. The word "depressed" is an adjective, which points to a condition of the subject, so it connects the subject to the object. The word "depressed" represents an emotion, which is a type of thought.

The reason for the depression — the emotion — is a belief. It appears to the self to be caused by the relationship (the object), but this is only a story that the self has created. The self attributes the emotion to the object.

"This conditioned 'I' is the real problem and cause for suffering," Guru-ma said.

Through a careful observation of my own life and the way the mind works, I could see that this subject-object falsehood had been the reason why I had run into the same types of situations over and over again. It became clear that my life experiences, like those of other people, were filled with encounters with some person who did not treat me fairly, or I had found anger wherever I turned, in situations and in people. There were countless examples of this subject-object principle in action. Life was an endless stream of them.

Apart from the belief of an individual "I" there is a unified consciousness, and in this state there are no subject-object relationships.

The self is not equipped to experience or perceive anything but fragmentation. To blame an emotion on another person or a situation is to live according to a belief in a fragmented reality. If you go through your life always believing that all your problems are "out there," you never stop to look inside of yourself.

The self takes ownership of emotions and their presumed causes. This must be clearly seen.

"If you want to go through this process of observing the tendencies and nature of the self," said Guru-ma, "stop believing you are an individual. As an individual you feel bad about yourself, blame yourself, or become insulted. Observe all that seems to happen from the perspective of the observer who is like the audience member watching a play. No matter how turbulent things become on the stage, the observer sits comfortably in her seat, unscathed, and watches the goings-on."

As the watcher, or observer, you may come to know that if the self does not get what it wants, it experiences suffering. The suffering comes from a desire for pleasure. In a relationship it says, "I am depressed over my relationship." In a situation it may say, "I am depressed that I do not have the same opportunities as my brother." But what is really going on is that the self is creating an excuse for its self-loathing, self-consciousness, and selfishness that comes from not meeting its projected desires. Suffering results from not feeling pleasure; it is not from a broken relationship, a lack of money, a person who slighted you, or your inability to make friends, because those are all objects that are being associated with the subject you call "I." Neither consciousness nor the body expresses a need for money, material goods, or fancy titles; only the self desires such things.

The self can seem to be self-reflexive, self-serving, self-aggrandizing, self-deprecating, self-centered, and self-conscious. It's all about me, me, me. The body requires shelter, but it is the egoic mind that jumps to make the claim "I need a house with a red roof and wooden floors." The self takes the physical need and directs it toward something that is a pleasing idea. Similarly, the body may sense the urge to put on a jacket, but it is the mind that says, "I refuse to wear the green one." There are endless ways that the self personalizes situations, people, places, and things by means of objectivization.

The body is a biological entity. It does not attribute feelings and emotions to its activities. It does not state that it is tired, worn-down, afraid, curious, lonely, lazy, ambitious, or sad. All it senses is a physiological occurrence. The self, on the other hand, interprets physiological needs according to its conditioning.

The self is constantly trying to make the outer world match the image it has built for itself as its identity. If the image is that I am a victim, I am misunderstood, I am being thwarted by others, I deserve new clothes, and so on, then the self will find or create an environment or adversary that will reinforce and give evidence to that story. When the self is depressed because it believes it, as an individual person, is a failure; then it seeks to blame someone or something. Psychologists' couches are filled with patients who blame their mothers for all their woes and failures. Placing blame on anything or anyone is part of the egoic belief system. The fact is that you are not the doer, and neither was your mother. Your woes appear with the objects you create in your role as the "I."

Do not try to change the mind — the fifth pillar

Knowing that the self is the source of suffering, I pondered what it would be like if I could erase the conditioning that had caused me so many problems throughout my life. Perhaps, I thought, this would be the solution to everyone's troubles! But how can the mind be erased. I decided to depart from Guru-ma's suggestion to seek the source of the "I," and instead I meditated on ways to be happier. It was a short-cut that was certain to work. Or so I thought.

One morning, well-rested following a night of sound sleep, I spritely walked off to breakfast brimming with happiness over having apparently found the answer to the escape from self. This newfound attitude brightened my mood. I assumed that the solution was only a matter of changing my attention from my familiar entanglement with anger and depression so that I would instead focus on happiness, love, and creativity.

I needed to tell someone — anyone — about my marvelous plan. So I entered the dining hall and positioned myself between an older couple that was visiting from a thousand miles away. At the first opportunity, completely uninvited, I inserted myself into their conversation and began to pontificate about the nature of the self, and how each person, as I pointed at each of them, was so full of his own emotions that he could not find happiness.

"It's only a matter of changing the mind," I informed them. "If you cannot control your mind, then you are destined to be on a wheel of pain and pleasure without chance for liberation."

What had begun as a lovely, relaxing morning for the couple was now disturbed by my rude and intrusive little speech. My enthusiastic lesson did not go over well, and the man and woman became quite agitated. But I continued to make things worse for them.

"Ah, you see that? Your very reaction," I told them, "serves to prove my point."

I smiled smugly as they picked up their plates, silently stood up, and moved to the other side of the room without looking back at me. Now I was convinced that I had something others did not have — a special insight into the way of things — and that they were not ready for such lofty teachings. I considered, perhaps, I had found the key to enlightenment at long last.

Another few weeks passed blissfully for me, and because I had not gone to one of Guru-ma's talks in quite some time, I decided to sit in one evening after dinner. The room was filled with visitors. They had eager but tired faces, and they hungered for words of wisdom, a masterful gaze, or at least to touch the hem of a sage. As a seasoned expert, I sat in the back where I had always been most comfortable.

A young European woman stood up, bowed, and glanced around the room, and then confidently proceeded to tell Guru-ma that she had realized her true nature and now wanted to know how she could share her knowledge and experiences with others.

"I had an experience of a bright light, like sunshine. The light was glowing and surrounding me, and there was this sound, too. It was like a deep hum, and I knew it was God." Smiling uncontrollably, she said, "My experience left me humble and feeling connected to everyone. Now I am overjoyed all the time. I know I have conquered my ego self. My mind is filled with nothing but bliss and good thoughts because I have moved on at last. I have learned how to focus only on the positive and let the negative simply wash over me. I am a part of God; I now know this in my heart."

Overjoyed with her feelings, she wiped her eyes, approached Guru-ma, and then touched her head to the sage's feet. My heart sank; not for the woman's emotions, but for something else. I saw myself in her. I saw my hubris and self-deceit. I recognized my own effort to be something other than what I am, trying to trade my conditioned mind for one that was reconditioned with better thoughts. I hung my head low, now seeing nothing but my feet and the floor. I glanced at the exit and wanted to walk away, but I dared not be a disruption. Guru-ma looked my way, but I tried not to meet her gaze.

When Guru-ma began to speak to this well-intentioned visitor she was stern but kind. Presently, she stared past the visitor and looked directly at me.

Guru-ma said, "The self very much enjoys thinking it has found all the answers, and it takes great pride in itself and its feelings of specialness and wisdom. It seems to get out of one trap and then right back into another one. Isn't it so? The self relishes knowing things, figuring it all out, and then proclaiming its achievement to the world." Then Guru-ma gently asked the woman, "Who is this 'I' that has changed and is now so filled with grace?"

Proudly, the woman smiled assuredly and pointed to her heart, saying, "Me. It is me, my guru."

Guru-ma then told her, "Leave the mind alone. What is this constant need to try to conquer the self, or to change it into something other than what it is? What is going on here?" And then she waited a long while for me to look up at her before saying, "The self has a certain nature that cannot be changed, so why try? When you try, you only reinforce it."

Guru-ma told a parable about a snake that slithered into a peaceful little village in a remote jungle. People were frightened, but had been taught not to kill or harm living beings, so they ran to the elder for help. The old man was renowned for his wisdom and ability to communicate with all living things. But he believed that people should make their own discoveries regardless of his insight.

"I will do what you like," the elder told the villagers, "but know this: The snake is a snake, and it acts as a snake."

More interested in getting rid of their problem than thinking about what the man had just told them, the villagers said, "We don't want to hear any philosophy from you. Just take action now! Tell that snake to act civilly."

The people were impatient, because the snake was eating small pets and threatening to bite anyone who went near it. It slithered in and out of people's huts as they clung to ceiling beams, scurried to the other side of the road in a panic, and huddled atop tables waiting anxiously for the animal to vacate their homes. The village elder methodically went from hut to hut looking for the snake before finding it outside, curled up beside a large boulder. The snake and the elder had a long conversation in which the serpent was told not to eat any more living creatures or bite the villagers. He told the snake that the villagers demanded that it take on a demeanor of friendship and altruism. Or else!

Three weeks later, the docile snake, which, by then, had become a beloved pet by all the villagers, was found dead in the middle of the road. It had starved to death. The people were saddened to have lost such a friendly and familiar part of their lives. They were beside themselves with grief, and could not understand what had happened. They had lost a pet whom they had been so joyful to know had changed its ways. With sadness weighing heavily in their hearts, they once again went to the elder, and now asked how this tragedy could have happened.

"You wanted the snake to be different from its natural self, so it died," said the old man. "A snake can only be a snake."

Guru-ma explained, "The self has a nature as well, and you cannot change it. You can try to distract it. You can recondition it, and you can entertain it or dull it with chemicals, but its very nature is to be a reflection of tightly held beliefs and memories. Thus, it is self-serving, fearful, and forever seeking pleasure and the avoidance of pain. It knows fear when it believes it is threatened, and it is constructed of thoughts such as greed, envy, hate, violence, lust, attachment, kindness, sadness, elation, vengeance, helpfulness, friendliness, interest, creativity, exploration, caring, the desire to help, and all the rest, comprising the entire spectrum of feelings and attributes. This is the self's very nature, and it will go on believing in certain ideas to preserve, promote, perpetuate, and validate itself."

The self is only a belief, a mirage. If you try to change it, then you will at best create a better mirage. But it will remain a mirage.

"So, leave the self alone," Guru-ma said once more. "Do not try to change it or make it better. See it for what it is. Watch it and understand its place. That's all you can do. The ego mind will always be the ego mind; it will always remain a belief until you eventually realize that you are not the body and that you exist without any identities or attachments. Trying to quiet the mind is itself a mind exercise. Neither psychology, spirituality, positive thinking, alcohol, imagination, drugs, entertainment, yoga, kundalini, exercise, nor mindfulness meditation will do anything to change the nature of the ego mind. You are not the self; leave it at that. It is the identification with the self and body that needs to be known. When this happens, the false belief of reality will dissipate on its own."

Yet another lesson in humility had come to me that day. I had seen in the visitor what I had failed to see in myself. I had fooled myself into thinking that I had changed my sense of self into something that was new and free. I had not changed my mind nor achieved anything permanent at all, as evidenced by the fact that I was left deflated and ashamed.

Two or three days of sulking had passed before I admitted to myself that I needed to return to Guru-ma's initial advice: "Ask yourself, 'Who am I?'" I felt like a neophyte, and fell back into a familiar depression. Diving deeper into the depths of self-loathing, I took a long, lumbering walk along a foothill path to be alone with my thoughts. I sat down on a patch of grass and stared out at the horizon, determined to go after this sense of depression as I had done with the emotion of anger. I made no effort to analyze, judge, or criticize myself, and I took Guru-ma's advice to heart — that my sense of self was nothing more than a belief.

It wasn't until I had awoken the next morning that it occurred to me that my chronic depression — an overpowering and sometimes debilitating emotion I had known for my whole life — resulted from the dissatisfaction of not being able to derive pleasure out of life. I came to know that this sense of a self is forever looking for pleasure, and, alternatively, how to avoid pain. It was the theme of all life for all people in all places. This pursuit of pleasure and avoidance of pain creates an endless, tiresome cycle of elation and suffering that are two sides of the same coin.

While this discovery was helpful in understanding the nature of the self, I knew that I still had been perceiving the world through the eyes of this same self, and I once again became frustrated in my inability to conquer it. I even considered leaving the ashram over a deep-seated disgust for an idea — a goal of enlightenment — that seemed hopeless, foolish, and impossible to grasp. The whole affair tortured me and tensed up my body. I wondered whether years and months of my short life had been bound up in futility.

The self is only a belief — the sixth pillar

Was it possible that my entire life had been lived in the shadow of a belief that I had called "me"? It became clear why most people would not want to face this problematic truth. Once this is known, then a reaction becomes necessary in the form of a readjustment, denial, reconditioning, or an awakening.

I tried to be devoid of any investment in the self and all identities when I inquired into the question "Who am I?" There was nothing but silence staring back at me. What could be the answer? Where was this "I" that I had for so long considered the center of my existence?

I retreated into silence for quite some time after I realized through observation that the self is a construct. It's not that all thoughts disappeared or that I had come to live in absolute bliss, but rather that it became clearer that I had been conditioned to make an image of a self that was identified with a body.

I looked in the mirror one morning just after climbing out of bed. Who was looking back at me? I saw a form with a familiar face, but the identities of a son, brother, and seeker of Truth were not there. But who was there? I was seeing a form, an expression that was somehow appearing out of consciousness. I tried to listen to the body to hear whether it spoke to me, but it did not. It did not tell me whether it was happy, sad, excited, depressed, angry, ambitious, or wanting for anything at all. These emotions existed only in the self. Other than sensations, there was no hint of desires or memories being reported by this biological being called a body.

I walked outside and wandered around until I found a spot in the center of the lawn where a bench overlooking a little pond awaited me. This particular day was especially teeming with activity, because a religious celebration was being held not far from the ashram. Visitors to the area decided to come to the ashram as part of their holiday experience, and they spent the day roaming the grounds, listening to Guru-ma, eating in the dining hall, and meditating in large groups. I decided I would listen to what people were saying.

On a bench a meter away from me a middle-aged man and his friend sat down to talk. One of them took out a map of the area and began pointing to various attractions that they could visit.

"This shrine," said the man, "is beautiful. I have been there before, two years ago. It was far too crowded at that time, but if we go early in the morning we will be alright."

"How far away is it?" asked the man's friend. "I don't want to walk for hours and wind up exhausted before the day starts."

"Not far. Look here," said the man while running his finger along his map. "There is a little tram we can take more than halfway."

"Perfect," said his friend. "I do not like those trams, but this is much easier."

The two men stood up and walked away, discussing the fair, but not exceptional, quality of food at the ashram and that some of the buildings were in need of repair.

As I listened to conversations like these, it became apparent to me that the self is continually providing commentary and weighing all actions on their merits of whether they will bring pleasure or cause discomfort. Is it possible to live one's life without such commentary? Does the body actually care or take notice of whether a building has peeling paint, or whether it will have to walk a far distance some time in the future? No, these are the petty concerns of the self — a belief system that is fearful of the future based upon one's past conditioning. One person is conditioned to complain about the price of a taxi ride, while another thinks nothing of it.

Each person whom I listened to expressed criticisms, compliments, and judgments about all sorts of things. The people around me were obsessed with, and unavoidably blinded by, conditioned minds full of opinions, wishes, and desires. The self was running the show.

With open eyes and ears, I was hearing my own sense of self in every voice around me. I was hearing my complaining and my useless, persistent preoccupations and fears. While there are practical reasons for thinking, I noticed that most thoughts are not about how to do something, but rather what people find important, unimportant, fun, boring, pleasant, beautiful, ugly, or difficult. Do any of these thoughts have to do with the practicality of living, eating or keeping safe from the elements?

Having spent the day without uttering a single word to anyone, I discovered that most of what is said comes from the self; the body has no opinion. But who is it that takes notice of this? Who sits quietly and observes the play? Who is this "I" who is aware of the self's character?

The self, the sense of "I," is a mirage, a shadow, or any other term you want to call it. When you continue to look for this "I," you cannot actually get hold of it or even find much benefit to it. It is comprised of thoughts that have coalesced into a belief, shared with others, defended, proffered, cherished, and clung onto. But do not gloss over these words, because if you do you may miss the very crux of all conflict — not only conflict in the world, but conflict within you as well. The self defends itself, sometimes to the very death of the physical body. People go off to war, stage protests, fight over property, battle with their neighbors or spouses, throw fits of jealous rage, and die for religious beliefs. Common to all of these acts is an "I" that is utterly convinced that the body is its true home and essence, and therefore must be protected against all unwanted ideas, perceived threats, and imagined insults. This conditioned mind is steeped in the belief that you are an individual encased in a physical body, because it is blinded to the wholeness of all there is.

While entertaining the character of the self, a thought about my father occurred to me. When I was a child, a long time friend of my father's came to visit one evening. Like my father, this man was a fisherman and often had plenty of time to think while his boat sat anchored in the ocean waiting for the day's catch to swim into his nets. My father's friend was particularly interested in politics and the oppression so many people were facing while a foreign government ruled the country. I listened as the man passionately told my father that he had joined a certain group bent on overthrowing the occupiers. He wanted my father to join his cause, which was the real purpose of his visit.

"We believe in justice and know that we are right," the man said with great conviction. "And you know it too," he said, slamming his fist on the table.

Sitting outside of our house that evening, as the light from the lanterns flickered, the faces of the men, sweaty and flushed, looked ominous to me. Through my childish eyes, being closer to the flame, our visitor's expression seemed harsh and mean, sending shivers of fear into me. I could not tell if he was a friend or foe, and I ran to my father, jumped into his lap, and pulled one of his arms around my chest.

My father sat thinking about what his friend had just said, but did not answer right away. For a moment, all that could be heard was the rustling of life in the jungle. Then my father took a long drag on his cigarette, and said, "Beliefs can get you killed."

While as a child I had very little understanding of the political situation under discussion, my father's comment had stuck in my memory. As a six-year-old, I found his words odd and almost poetic. I didn't know all of what they implied, but I wondered how a belief — something so intangible — could be referred to as deadly.

Our visitor eventually became frustrated at not being able to convert my father to his cause. He picked up his pack of cigarettes, drank his last sip of tea, and left our house in a most unhappy state. As he stepped off our front porch, he turned to my father and said, "I hope you'll consider what this means and what you must do."

What did it mean? Sitting at the ashram, so many years later, I thought about this exchange between my father and his friend. They were discussing ideas, beliefs. I now knew that ideas were thoughts, and that people found thoughts to be charged with right, wrong, good, bad, or healthy; they were said to be virtuous, ethical, immoral, exciting, or unhealthy. But where were these thoughts? Who was having them, and who was affected by them? They could not be seen, and they were fleeting, yet the whole world clung tightly to their meaning. One's political or religious convictions could mean the difference between living and dying. How strong were beliefs? The lives of billions of people are swayed by thoughts that have accreted to form their senses of self. A belief system called the "I" is created out of nothing but thoughts, and this invisible, transitory, changeable thing has such great potential for either violence or redemption. This fact of life seemed so insane to me.

Although the self is a belief, I realized that it is not to be taken lightly. It influences life at every turn. As a bundle of conditioned thoughts, the self finds it frightening, inconceivable, and/or impossible to surrender its own beliefs and perspective so that the Truth may be realized. It does not welcome the Truth in most people. The "I' sense stubbornly stands between the body and consciousness, and it is the grand purveyor of most suffering. Its impact and weight is held in place by both the believer and others who have their own beliefs. People live and die, prosper and fail, and suffer and rejoice based on a bundle of thoughts particular to their own conditioning.

The center of most people's world, the self, as a judge, commentator, and conjurer of fear, has created a false imprisonment. It is the self that informs you that it — the "I" — is important and indispensable. It is much like a narcissist who is continually misleading you and creating a path of destruction and confusion, while ever reminding you, "You can't get rid of me, because I am the leader, and I am essential to your world and happiness. I am your only hope for salvation."

If you are fortunate enough to learn that the self is no more than a belief, you must either have the courage and desire to realize its true nature and let its central role fade away, or do what most people do, and that is to continue on in misery, delusion, pain, suffering, anger, envy, and disappointment until the end of their days. You may even face the fact of all the shortcomings, quirks, and ugliness of this little self called "me," and then set these aside as if they are not part of you at all, and continue to live your life with a sense of isolation and otherness.

There are many ways that people attempt to quell, ignore, and avoid their suffering, but it is only the very rare who have the desire and fortitude to find that which comes prior to the pettiness, individualism, fragmentation, ideas, mental conditioning, and accretion of thoughts.

As long as the belief of a self persists, you will remain affixed to a cycle of pain and pleasure. Those who do not realize the Truth continue to fill their lives with endless distractions and noise. They distract themselves from knowing themselves. Such is the power of the mind that has been tainted by the ego.

One of the first things that I had ever heard Guru-ma say was that the self is a ball of tightly wound, conditioned ideas. This led me to question: "Is this all that I am?" How could this be? Am I only a collection of ideas? Certainly, I thought at the time, there must be something more to me. Eventually I would learn that all of my actions, thoughts, hopes, desires, words, and expressions were pre-programmed by the conditioning of the mind. A major part of this conditioning led me, like most others, to believe that I was no more than the body and the world that I created with my impressions and interpretations.

"As long as you are looking out at this world through the lens of the self," Guru-ma said, "You do not know who you are."

As you read these words, you must come to realize that you are not what you think yourself to be. Some people who are exposed to this idea may be hit so hard that they lapse into a depression or, as a matter of the self's attempt at defense, a predictable state of denial. They may be lost without a compass, without an anchor to keep them from drifting away from their own sense of reality. Or they may try to shy away from the truth of what they are. But any attempt to escape is as illusory or real as the fact of the "I" itself. Who is escaping from what? And why? This is what you must find out for yourself. If you have a strong desire to know, then it is up to you to get to the bottom of it.

Perhaps, like me, you will be one of the few who is hopelessly driven to pursue the Truth of your nature, undaunted to discover the self for what it is. Perhaps you will be the next one who lays out the faults, shortcomings, pettiness, and ugliness of the self, and exposes it to the light of day so that its image is burned away by full awareness. This is sometimes referred to as the death of the ego, but since the ego does not exist except as a belief, there is nothing to die or be killed.

You are not what the self presents to you. It is only an elaborate, powerful, persistent, and stubborn belief.

Language is only a pointer
— the seventh pillar

Since the earliest of days of my self-searching, I wanted nothing else in this confusing life other than to know the true nature of this being called "I." I was convinced this would take hard work and thinking about the deeper meaning of the words that rolled so easily off the lips of Guru-ma. Over and over again, I clung to every utterance that she made, listening closely to every syllable, and then parsing each sentence. Certainly, I thought, there must be a hidden message in her clever words. There was even a part of me that looked to find a flaw in her statements — some contradiction or hint of ignorance.

I hung onto Guru-ma's every sentence so closely that I soon became full of knowledge about the nature of the Truth and the process of realization. In the long run, this brought me no closer to my ultimate desire of knowing my true nature. Instead, it drove me deeper and deeper into the abyss of ideas. The more I had fought to understand the wholeness of life through words and concepts, trying to grasp new and intriguing teachings, the more I had reinforced a sense of individuality. I began to identify with statements, ideas. I had been repeatedly told to surrender all of these notions and to stop hanging onto the words, but the mind clamped onto concepts with great alacrity and pride.

"These words are no more than concepts; they are not the Truth. They are only pointers," my teacher told me on more than one occasion.

But throughout my earliest steps on the path to finding myself, I had no way of listening. I was hearing, but not listening. The self had latched onto how sentences were formed, and how certain important principles were communicated. I often found myself trying to catch my teacher in a mistake, identifying her by her statements, and judging her by her specific use of words. I challenged paradoxes and the way she stated ideas, seeming to contradict herself at times.

But she did not seem to care that I was holding her to an image of my own making.

One day I went to visit Guru-ma as she was helping prepare lunch for 200 people. Giant vats of steaming food filled the air with a dense cloud so that she was at times barely visible to me. The clanging of pots, pans and utensils compelled the kitchen workers to shout above the noise. I followed Guru-ma around as she industriously went from station to station checking everyone's progress. Then, in the midst of the utter chaos, she stopped to look at me.

"What do you want?" she shouted.

She scurried off to the other side of the kitchen to fetch a jar of spices while I stood still. I was taken aback at what she had yelled at me, wondering what kind of attitude was being displayed by such a saintly figure. As she disappeared into a large pantry, I stared off into space until she returned. Next, I watched her call out commands to an army of helpers who were now plating the food for scores of guests, visitors, and devotees who had begun to enter the dining hall.

Four or five kitchen workers rushed by me carrying heavy trays of food while I still stood transfixed and in their way. Guru-ma wiped her hands on her apron, took me by the arm, and ushered me to a corner of the turbulent room. I wondered what was going through her mind, or whether any thoughts ever occurred to her at all. I tried to read her facial expressions and body language. She seemed so human and fallible, and nothing like I had heard such sages were certain to be, or what their followers had described. Standing before me I did not see a sage, but instead a disheveled woman stained with food, and perspiring from the intense heat of the kitchen.

With a steady temperament, and a great humanness in her demeanor, Guru-ma patiently watched me as thoughts raced through my mind. I was trying to figure out this person who was one day stern and another day lighthearted. To some visitors she was brutally honest, and to others she was soft and nurturing. In her presence, or by her gaze, there were no instantaneous transmissions of enlightenment, nor were there any shocks of electricity when she would touch your head or casually brush by you. And so she reached out and placed her hand on my arm. I felt nothing but warmth and compassion.

I was thinking that, despite what flowery, mystical, or saintly statements had been attributed to this generally placid, attractive woman, Guru-ma was no less or more ordinary than any other woman one might see in any village going about her business. When she talked, her arms and hands were light and free-flowing. Her face, with the slightest hint of wrinkling around the eyes and mouth, was ever-radiant. I studied her long hair, blacker than night and pinned back, giving her a youthful appearance. Even in this very moment, in the commotion of the lunch hour, Guru-ma's countenance was one of strength and quietude.

I did not know what to expect from her as she pulled me aside to talk. I had seen that, as a guru, she was given to yelling at people from time to time. She sometimes seemed to be impatient with visitors who cared to ask her no more than questions about her own experiences or how she viewed the world. At those moments her answers were terse and halting. She had little time for such trivia.

I thought about what she had shouted at me a minute earlier — "What do you want?"

"Your questions are coming from the self," Guru-ma said. "You have a mind that is searching, searching, searching, for answers that have nothing to do with you, rather than desiring to find the Truth that is you. If you want to ask me a serious question, then go ahead. Otherwise, we have nothing more to say to one another."

Yes, she seemed very human at times, and devoid of mystery or mysticism, except to say it remained a mystery as to what she was perceiving reality to be. She did not even prefer to sit on a dais to give her talks, and here she was, elbow to elbow with all the other kitchen workers, up to her neck in flour and spices. Guru-ma was a constant reminder to each visitor and devotee that there is no hierarchy, no separations according to assumed levels of consciousness, or any other sorts of nonsense. Yet I remained intimidated by her. Or was this only how the ego mind tended to see her?

Despite calls for her assistance over by the stove, Guru-ma stood patiently beside me as if she had all the time in the world to devote to my needs. I do not know whether it was from the heat or the noise, but I felt unsteady on my feet, and I stared down at the floor, speechless.

She placed her fingers under my chin, slowly lifted my head, and said, "When you look at me, you see the expression, separate from what you perceive is 'you.' You see only the parts, only the expression, only individuals. Isn't this so? And so you go on creating images of everything, including what you see as this body standing before you, trying to help you. You study my face and body, you see a form, and you differentiate it from the form through which you sense the world. You may continue to do this for as long as it pleases you, but if you are sincere, then you will use my words not as a means to assess me or learn a teaching or technique, but instead to probe the recesses of your mind until you realize what you are. The mind must abandon the objects and words, even the object that you perceive is me. Then allow the mind to fold inward upon itself, and then you will notice what has been here all along. You and I are the same, but at this moment it is only I who knows this. Find out who you are."

I knew at that instant that I had been stubborn, foolish, ignorant, arrogant, and attached to my beliefs. I had been hanging onto words, trying to figure out my teacher, and memorizing principles. I had been trying to understand important ideas expressed in a language that my mind hoped to grasp through study and deconstruction of meaning. None of this had anything to do with finding the Truth about myself; it was all a distraction — the self doing what it was wont to do.

Guru-ma said, "The self relishes puzzles, mysteries, and word play. The Absolute is not to be found in such ideas."

"The Absolute?" I questioned. "This is still an abstract idea for me. You talk about it, but it is a word, like all other words."

"Guru-ma! Guru-ma!" yelled a worker from across the room as she struggled to balance a heavy bowl of soup over a cauldron, "please help!"

I looked at the woman and her expression of fright, but Guru-ma did not budge. Her full attention remained on me. Just in time, another kitchen worker ran to the woman's aide and her crisis was averted. I turned my attention back to my teacher.

"Exactly," she said as if no one but the two of us were in the room. "The Absolute is only a word, an idea. By being distracted, you have separated yourself from the Absolute, and so all things for you are broken into an infinite array of ideas, images, forms, and words. I can tell you about the Absolute, but what will it really mean to you or anyone else? Words are like a finger pointing at the moon. The moon is not the finger."

Language cannot explain or convey the Absolute reality that lies behind the mind and all expressions arising out of consciousness, because the Absolute is not an object. The Absolute is prior to consciousness, unchanging, unbounded, indescribable, unexplainable, still, silent, and non-cancellable. The movement of consciousness arises out of the Absolute, and it is this movement that creates life as we know it, with all the expressions, forms, thoughts, ideas, and action.

At the most, all that words can provide is a hint of what may be realized when the "I" no longer identifies with the body. But this mental understanding — the learning — is a trap, because it is not a realization through anything other than second-hand information. You must go further and make your own, first-hand realization.

"You may describe all the properties, textures, temperature, and sensations of water, but this cannot convey the true experience of immersion into water. Isn't it so?" asked my teacher. "The state that you are seeking is already here; it is already you. In silence you know it, but there is no silence in your mind, because it is consumed with the self," she said. "Be quiet."

This was a difficult lesson for me, a person who had spent years trying to use my mind to figure everything out and get to the bottom of things. Like so many others, I had been preoccupied with mentally wrestling with human nature.

Guru-ma said, "All language is from memory; nothing that language describes is happening at this very moment that we call 'now.' Use it as a guide, not a doctrine or a dogma. Even the words of the self-realized guru are fragmented and limited, because language cannot be otherwise. Stop hanging on my words; I am nobody. Language is language. Leave it at that!"

I had learned that all of what you read, including these very words, are from the past and no longer alive. They are ideas, not actualities; and they are not yours at all. An idea or description, even of the Absolute, is not to be taken as knowledge to memorize or to live by.

Guru-ma led me outside into a shady courtyard. Compared to the noisy kitchen, the quietude was otherworldly, and not another soul was in sight. With a raspy voice following an hour of shouting over the din of the commotion inside, Guru-ma said, "Mine are not words of authority and instruction. They are not prescriptions for a belief system or a better 'you.' They point to something that language has no way of transmitting. It cannot be repeated enough that you must find out for yourself if anything that you read or hear is true."

And then she wiped off her hands, marched back into the building, and left me alone in the quiet. Try as I might, for the longest time I could not remember anything she had told me that day. Her words had vaporized into steam; only the impact remained.

Language is all we have to communicate anything, whether it's the language of words, art, dance, sounds, signs, facial expressions, symbols, metaphors, body postures, or symbols. But, you must be careful with language, because it is usually misleading, incomplete, paradoxical, misunderstood, and even self-contradictory.

If you want an example of how language fails, perform one simple exercise: Try to explain the nature of absolute silence. Or try to explain the present, without any reference to the past. The instant you begin to speak, the present is already gone, and a new present exists.

Not more than a week later, I was listening to a visitor ask Guru-ma what was behind the self and consciousness. I could not imagine what she would say to the woman.

"You say there is an indescribable stillness, a space," said the visitor. "I don't understand."

"The Absolute lies behind all expression and potential. But to say it is behind is not even the truth. It is all that exists, the backdrop, the foundation, the infinite, the composition, and the predecessor. But what use is it to speak of this? First find out who wants to know such things."

I did not stay to hear the rest of the lesson. I walked away and recalled what it had been like for me when I first heard these words. What can they possibly mean to one whose attention has for so long been set firmly upon the objects of the self and whose references are, by default, all rooted in the past? What can words mean for one who is continually objectifying the world? What occurs when you hold tightly to concepts and painstakingly try to analyze their meaning? Perhaps you may come away with the impression that there is a state of totality, but in trying to understand this you may become fixated upon the word "state," or you may have a preconceived idea of what totality means. Then you may conclude that the Absolute is a state and is temporal, because all states are conditions. Or you may place your attention on the word "behind," and try to imagine the Absolute as something that exists spatially. Words are faulty because they are pieces of the whole; they describe aspects and qualities. So, do you cling to the words anyway and abandon the desire for the Truth, or do you look past the failure of language in order to steadfastly inquire into your own nature to determine for yourself whether there is indeed an Absolute?

The lesson I had learned was to let language point me in the direction of my true nature; it must serve as a map, not an answer.

In the end, we have no tool with which to communicate who we truly are once the self is discovered to be no more than a belief. This is why so many who have realized their true nature default to silence. Through the ages, monks, nuns, renunciants, ascetics, gurus, and others have retreated far from the things of humankind to be away from the spoken word. They were all making an attempt to uncover what has been obscured by the mind that is so steadfastly rooted in objects such as language.

Silence says it all.

The seeker must stop seeking — the eighth pillar

Early one morning I was walking toward the front gate of the ashram to watch the newest stream of pilgrims on their way to see Guru-ma. Here and there a weary traveler would perk up as he set his eyes on the manicured grounds ahead of him. He would pass through the gate with renewed vigor and expectation of something magical lying in wait. There were a few couples as well — Western men and women, smartly dressed, with the men in white linen suits and matching white hats, and the women were cloaked in loose-fitting, gauzy gowns and uncomfortable, fashionable shoes. They steadily stepped out of dilapidated taxis, ready for this, the next stop on their tour of this remote part of the world. Each visitor had an eager smile and a look of promise and hope on his or her face.

I was about to head back to the main hall where Guru-ma would soon entertain the latest congregation of visitors when I saw a familiar figure coming up the path. I could hardly believe what my eyes were showing me — it was the kindly woman I had met on the train so long ago — the one who had been a devotee of Guru-ma and who had led me to this place. I rushed to the gate to welcome her in, and to my surprise, her face lit up with recognition. After a warm hug, we strolled arm-in-arm onto the grounds.

"You made it after all," she said to me, taking my hand in hers.

"It was you who had changed my fate," I said.

"We both know that's not true," she said with a laugh.

We walked up to the main building and took a seat on a bench in the colonnade where we could enjoy the sunshine without having it beat directly down on us.

"Here we are where we left off," she said. "The two of us on a bench."

"Nothing really changes, I guess."

"Look at you. I don't see the same boy with such a knot in his stomach. Perhaps you have found what you were looking for."

"Have you?" I asked.

"Clever," she said. "I meant to say that Guru-ma must have passed your test for legitimate teachers, no?"

"I have to apologize for the way I went on with my jaded opinions of gurus and priests," I said.

"I was only teasing. But I must say that you seem so much more relaxed and settled down. It's nice to see."

I realized how much I had missed my friend's soothing voice and inner peace. Sitting beside this woman warmed the heart in a way that words fail to describe. There was something much deeper than met the senses. There was a wisdom beyond her words and years, as if behind those big brown eyes was the infinite well that Guru-ma had called the Absolute.

As we gazed at one another, I saw myself and the world in her. She smiled and ran the back of her fingers down my cheek.

"The desire to know one's true nature has been called the razor's edge," she said softly. "It's a wonderful expression, don't you think?"

I nodded, but in all honesty I was not certain what she meant.

She explained, "It is the delicate line between too much and too little desire and effort. And there is a razor's edge between the search for the ultimate and the search to become something. The razor's edge, too, is that balancing point for one who has realized his true nature but lives fully in this world of expression. The Truth is right here, and yet we look for it as if it were somewhere else, forever separating ourselves from the whole. The process is a paradox; effort creates more problems, and yet not enough effort means no success. All of what is sought — the Absolute truth — is always present, so in reality, seeking is a futile endeavor."

At this point, several people came by and sat along the low wall bordering the colonnade to eavesdrop. Perhaps they recognized my friend who had spent so many summers visiting the ashram. Normally I would have felt invaded by penetrating eyes and ears, but suddenly I did not care. In invited the lesson that was unfolding before my friend even had a chance to wash up and put her bags away.

"Does it take any effort to pay attention?" she asked. "By keeping the mind out of the process, attention is the way to realize your true nature. Ultimately, you must give up chasing the idea of self-realization and enlightenment. Of course, this at first seems paradoxical. How can it not be, when the mind makes a concept out of everything, and, in this case, tries to grasp something that is prior to the mind itself?"

In less than a minute, my beautiful, glowing friend had summarized my long and tortuous journey to know myself. A lump formed in my throat as I gazed at her, realizing that she had been one of the most important gurus in my life. I told her this, but she seemed disinterested in sentimentality.

"Do not make anything special of me," she said with a smile. "I am nothing, least of all your guru."

Suddenly my friend let go of my hands and looked up to see Guru-ma coming our way with a small entourage. I stood up, looked at Guru-ma, and then back at my friend. And then, with the help of one of her devotees, and her walking stick, Guru-ma approached my friend, bowed, and then painstakingly knelt upon the ground to touch her feet. My friend placed her hand on Guru-ma's head and then pressed her palms together in a greeting. Guru-ma returned the gesture and then, without a word ever being spoken by anyone, continued on her way into the main building.

Unmoved by what had just happened, my friend continued where she had left off, "All expressions are manifested out of the great consciousness, and permeating these expressions of you and I and the plants, the trees, the sun, the moon, these people sitting here listening in, and every guru imaginable, is that great consciousness. There is no distinction between the guru and the beggar, between you and me, between me and that stone in the garden. All is one undivided whole of existence; this is you. You must know that it is all you. Seize this, claim it! The guru is you, is it not? This makes seeking after anything an exercise of the mind. But it is all you and has never been otherwise."

I looked at my friend in wonder and said, "It is you I should call by the name of Guru-ma."

She said, "You can call me by whatever name you'd like, but if you look upon me with awe, then to you I shall remain an image and you shall remain an individual."

My friend allowed her words to sink in.

"Please continue," I said.

"You came here as a seeker, as do we all," she said. "But it is time to stop seeking."

I tilted my head as a puppy would do upon hearing a sound that it had never heard before.

She said, "Even the act of seeking is an error at some point. The mind has been trained and formed so that we believe we get what we want because we work hard for it. Even thieves learn to work hard. They want to pull off a heist, so they begin scheming and planning. Their effort is no less earnest than that of the student who yearns to one day become a doctor. Whatever one's hobby, occupation, or service, the methodology is the same, based on learning — trying to achieve a goal through the expenditure of time, energy, thought, planning, and strength of character. But when we speak of finding our true nature, we are not talking about a method. We are talking about observation, because this great attention will bring about a change and a realization. No movement is necessary. The mind is movement. Consciousness is movement. But the Absolute, which is behind all existence and the mind itself, is stillness, ever-present, ever you. You must be quiet and know it."

My gentle friend concluded, "Effort and desire are only needed to get you to the gate, which is to provide you with an understanding about what is going on. At first, it may help for most people to identify and talk about the self, consciousness, the Absolute, and other concepts, even to become convinced that you are not the body. However, merely to know about the form and existence of such things is not a realization of your true nature."

This is all my friend had to say for the moment, and I needed to let her words marinate inside of me.

We spent the rest of the morning together and shared a laugh over how I had travelled for hours in the wrong direction on my quest to find Guru-ma. It turns out there was no such thing as the wrong direction after all. At the end of our little reunion that morning, my friend set off to pay her respects to Guru-ma and enjoy her visit in the deep silence that was her.

You are not the doer, and nothing is mine or yours — the ninth pillar

It was a warm evening, nearly midnight, and few could sleep in the stagnant, humid air. Many had gone out onto the gardens in the hopes of catching the slightest breeze. Unable to rest, I tried to meditate, but was still too uncomfortable. So I sat on the edge of my bed and stared at the moonlight streaming in through the tiny window and falling at my feet.

Outside there were muffled voices coming from a small group of five or six devotees gathering on the lawn. In the center was Guru-ma in a lightweight white dress and holding her walking stick. She appeared as an apparition, and I strained my eyes to see that she was not. I put on my shoes and joined the party setting out on a long walk around the base of the nearby mountain.

The sky was a showcase of millions of stars dancing and glittering in a brilliant, wondrous and silent performance. Though the neck strained and ached from gazing heavenward, one could not resist to do so. Infinity enveloped all.

Guru-ma leaned heavily on one of her aides, placed one hand on her hip, and smiled so that her teeth shone in the darkness. She gazed up at the stars and wiped away beads of sweat forming on her brow. Though the sun had long ago set, the air and soil remained particularly warm, prompting two devotees bearing palm fronds to rush up to Guru-ma in an attempt to ease her discomfort. She waved them off, though, and those closest to her warned the others not to disturb her peace, so they fell several paces back, satisfied enough to trail behind in the darkness. Then she called for me to walk beside her, and we were most content to listen to the sound of our bare feet brushing against the dirt and tiny rocks on the dry path beneath us.

Far in the distance, with the stars reflecting off its surface, was the lake where I had spent so much time watching golden sunrises spread their light over the hills and trees on clear, dewy mornings. Someone from our group pointed at the still body of water, where a couple of boys were drifting aimlessly in a small boat. Their arms were draped over the edge of the vessel, and their hands were cutting through the glassy surface. Tiny ripples spread out in all directions. We all gathered around to watch the shadowy spectacle.

"You," Guru-ma said deliberately, "are *not* the doer. Like that boat, there is a body that moves from here to there, and all the expressions of life seem to take action within your world. The body is affected by this great movement of consciousness that also affects all other bodies, nature, animals, and objects. But when consciousness causes this or that to occur, the self takes the credit or blame. See if this is true."

This truth, that there is no doer, is perhaps the most difficult to accept, because it cuts to the core of the self. The ego mind, after all, has positioned itself as the center of a person's universe — the creator, controller, decider, instigator, and leader.

"Success and failure are taken to heart, and the self claims either as its doing," Guru-ma said. "Who is ready to accept that the body and consciousness move along without any need for, or help from, the self? Who is left to say, "I have done this" when there is no self to make the claim? The body cannot speak to say that it is the doer, and the consciousness that drives the body and gives rise to all expressions has no need to make such a claim. The self is a belief, and, like a mirage, has no power or will at all."

These words — "I am not the doer" — perplex the self to the point where it continually fights to prove it is untrue. Try telling a stranger he is not the doer and find out how he responds! Such a statement is extremely upsetting, and is rejected out of hand by most human beings, even if they say they want to know the Truth. Even when they say they agree, they continue to act as though they are the doers!

The very existence of the egoic mind — the way it believes itself to be the center of all things — is thwarted by this reality. If they take it to heart that they are not the doers, people may consider their existence to be without purpose, responsibility, or hope. The news may be met with helplessness, hopelessness, nihilism, depression, anger, outcry, or denial, but all attempts to deny this are based only upon second-hand knowledge, ignorance, or self-deceit. It is the "I" who makes the fuss and presents the denial. Only when you find out for yourself, through an inquiry into the "I," is this truth of non-doership apparent.

Guru-ma explained, "All existence is in consciousness, giving rise to appearances that include coming and going, appearing and disappearing, birth and death, rising and falling, and finding and losing. Consciousness alone is the source of all that appears to create action, including the actions of the body and all of the objects, experiences, and lifeforms that people call "hers," "mine" or "yours." Consciousness brings about interactions between people and other people, between people and nature, and between people and objects. It is only because the mind objectifies everything that you believe that you are a separate entity from the whole fabric of totality. And in this separation you fail to see what is causing the doing and thinking."

You are not the doer. The body goes through actions, and the mind has thoughts, but consciousness creates these activities, not an "I" who is the perceived individual. In the simplest of explanations, consciousness stimulates and energizes the body to act, and then the self steps in and claims responsibility or blame for the action. Or the self can demand that it is to be rewarded, appreciated, punished, or respected. If bad behavior ensues, then other egoic minds, due to *their* own conditioning, will blame or scold what they believe is a "you." The world is filled with people blaming each other for powers beyond their control. In essence, they are blaming and crediting people for the conditioning they have received that has or has not brought them to what is termed rightful or wrongful action.

Decision-making and movements are directed by consciousness, not the mirage called the "I." How can a mere belief — a mirage — do anything?

All that *is* exists in a network — an interconnected, inseparable, flowing, dynamic and complex reality. How can an ocean wave claim that it is the doer, when it is inseparable from the movement and entirety of the whole ocean?

Even the *sense* of a self, an individual, arises after the doing is done. The grand illusion is that this individual sense has created the world, thoughts, actions, forms, relationships, and so on. It believes that it has attracted good luck and material possessions by means of willpower, prayer, wishes, or accident.

"Whether you consider yourself to be a murderer or a saint, or a unifier or divider, it is because you have been conditioned to this very point by a stream of ideas from authority figures, teachers, gurus, writers, artists, friends, neighbors, relatives, newspaper articles, books, and experiences," said Guru-ma. "If you think yourself to be a wonderful person who gives to the needy and makes soup for the sick, it is only conditioning — the effect of consciousness — that has made you so."

The self is wont to take credit for good deeds so that you, as a belief, feel superior to others, even if you believe yourself to be humble and altruistic.

Guru-ma left little entire group with one last idea that star-filled evening. She said, "The mistake of believing that you are the body and the thoughts with which you identify leads to the error of believing that you do anything of your own volition. Who is the 'I' that does anything? See if you can find this 'I.' If you search long and hard enough for it, the truth will become apparent."

Consciousness, as the movement behind all creation, including the creation of the mind and body, leads to all pursuits, actions, and conditions. But the "I" places itself at the center and, in doing so, experiences a perpetual cycle of frustration, exhilaration, creation, destruction, and suffering, because it can never actually step out of itself. Nor can it, for all its claims to being a doer, control the world around itself.

The guru is you; surrender to yourself — the tenth pillar

Before the season of the afternoon rains, I wandered through the gardens as scores of pilgrims brought gifts and greetings to Guru-ma. Each morning I would follow them as they made their way into the small, stark receiving room where she held her early meetings. Many fawned over her, kissed her feet, and brought her food. They prostrated themselves in her long shadow, and kneeled before her, desperately seeking something to uplift their spirits. They stared at the faint lines and enigmatic expressions on her face, and strained their minds over how she might be perceiving the world. What was this spectacle?

One morning, when one of these sweet and sincere devotees from the West came to sit near me, I asked him what was the source of his great attention on the guru. He smiled knowingly and bowed his head, eager to share his secret with me.

"This is called surrendering to the guru," the young man said softly. "I have given myself completely to her. This is what is required to reach illumination. The guru, by her grace, shall recognize the devotion of the aspirant and his willingness to surrender everything over to her as a sign of his readiness to be taken up into bliss. If grace smiles upon me, I may receive her *darshan* and immediately become enlightened by her gaze."

I nodded and smiled. The man's words were so sincere, hopeful, crisp and clear, and his intention pure and innocent. I was reminded of Guru-ma's words, still fresh in my mind from the previous week.

She said, "The guru is you. Yes, it is you. The guru appears out of the same Absolute that is you, and so the guru is everything that guides you. It may be a book, a teacher, a situation, an inspiring or troubling motion picture, a shocking experience, a stage play, a tragedy, a puppy, a cow, or another person — even your child or a so-called enemy. But this idea of surrender is so often misunderstood. Surrender is about giving up the egoic mind; letting it go. Surrender this small self and the wagonload of thoughts that impair your vision. Surrender is giving up all closely held thoughts and tendencies of thinking to realize what you are and what you have always been."

I had discovered for myself that the self is the instrument that brings despair; it is the agent of suffering. It is but a belief that keeps people in a state of inertia, cycling from happiness to suffering and back again, so many times that you one day become sick of it.

Guru-ma had on more than one occasion told me, "The road that leads you toward your own true nature is despair." I do not know whether this was something she had said to others, but it was definitely something that I needed to look into.

When she had first told this to me, I was too entrenched in my own beliefs to realize what she meant. But now I was in the right frame of mind, and I thought about this for quite some time until it became apparent that desire is a result of conditioning, and despair and desire share the same mother.

"Consciousness must bring you, the "I," to the point of giving up. That which must be surrendered is the belief that has been with you all your life — that you are nothing more than the mind and the body and all manner of identities and assumed possessions," Guru-ma told me. "To transfer this responsibility to a man or woman who appears as a guru is to misunderstand the very nature of surrender. Personality worship will get you nowhere. I cannot make you realize anything, and I cannot surrender the 'I' on your behalf."

Eventually you learn — because consciousness brings you to this stage — that effort takes you only so far, and then it outlives its purpose. It keeps you firmly in the cycle of pleasure and pain. Even effort must be surrendered. Effort is the action of the mind that is borne out of the desire to achieve or obtain something, and only the self engages in such pursuits for reward or to avoid suffering. The egoic mind tries hard to control the situation, and it suffers disappointment for doing so. When at long last you learn this, and are ripe for it, you come to realize how in vain have been your efforts — your intense study, prostrating before the guru or staring at his or her photograph, endless reading, judging, memorizing holy passages, trying hard to pay attention, and attempting to be more aware. Behind all of these acts of a desire to become enlightened or a superior being is the self, fearing that it will not achieve this state. This fear is rooted in a conditioned thought called expectation.

Beware of the thought that says, "I want." I want enlightenment. I want a way out. I want to be the same as my guru. I want the guru to transfer enlightenment to me. All iterations of "I want this or that" are thoughts clinging in vain to an object. They are the essential "I" turned outward, but they must eventually turn inward, leading you to intense observation of who you are without fixation on a goal.

When the thought, "I want enlightenment" is present, then it is the same as "I don't want suffering in my life." But you must find out who this "I" is that wants such things. All of its efforts are involved in trying to push life in a desired direction. This is ultimately why it suffers. This pushing about is due to conditioning that informs you that this is the way to get what you want.

What you have read of my story thus far is merely more conditioning, and now you have been exposed to the suggestion that there is no goal to be achieved. Find out if this is true by means of observation with complete attention. And beware of observation itself. Observation does not include observing a guru and then trying to copy his/her actions. Instead, it has to do with listening to what is said, and then seeing if it is so for you by means of your own observation of the wholeness of existence, without the judgmental self. Take an inventory of who you are.

The self defines and categorizes what it perceives into likes, dislikes, good, bad, ugly, pretty, light, dark, and so on. Its world is that of fragmentation, not wholeness. As such, it can be said to have tunnel vision. It is immature and judgmental. So, what will you do after discovering this? Will you set off to practice non-judgment as a virtue and path to enlightenment? This is yet another trap — a common misinterpretation of what non-judgment implies. A lack of judgment is a byproduct of pure observation in the present, without the interference of the self. It is being aware without choice.

Practicing non-judgment is but another attempt by the self to achieve a desire. While it may make you get along better with others, and to be a nicer, more considerate person, non-judgment is not a path to awakening to the true nature of who and what you are.

Consciousness has brought you to this point. It is not luck, nor is it hard work, nor good or bad karma, nor the effort to be a better person. Consciousness — the flow of life and seed of expression — dictates the shape, size, outcome, obstacles, and direction of life. This includes where you — the expression of life in the form of the body and mind — are now, and how you got to this point. It also moves you to desire freedom from the mind, or whatever else it is that you want.

So, what is it that you need to surrender to bring you to know your true nature?

You are that which you seek — the eleventh pillar

As we slowly walked around the base of the mountain overlooking the ashram far below, Guru-ma stopped to listen to two young men lost in conversation several paces behind us. They were discussing liberation from the mind, prompting Guru-ma to shake her head and blurt out, "The concept of liberation is preposterous."

The two men looked at her with puzzled expressions. She had taken the wind out of their sails and stymied their discussion.

Guru-ma said, "What is wrong with this concept?"

No one replied.

A small circle of people had gathered around, eager to soak in what Guru-ma was about to say. Coming to join us was an old, weathered man, who had been a gardener at the ashram for more than thirty years. Breathing heavily, he sat down on a boulder and listened intently to our conversation.

"Is there a clearer way to explain this?" someone asked Guru-ma.

The old man grunted, stood up, and used his walking stick to push his way into the center of our little meeting. He wore nothing but a loin cloth, and I had never taken much notice of him before. Once in a while I had seen him weeding the gardens and cleaning the terraces of debris, but his quiet, old demeanor had made him nearly invisible to everyone. This unassuming man with sun-baked skin and a short white beard kept to himself, but his eyes bored into you and his words were sharp if you cared to engage him. Suddenly I was now seeing a sage where I had moments before seen a groundskeeper trying to keep pace with us as we walked higher and higher around the mountain.

Guru-ma backed out of our circle and allowed the man to speak in his raspy, tired voice.

"Who wants to be liberated?" he asked.

Several people raised their hands and smiled. Then they looked to Guru-ma for approval. She remained expressionless.

"Very good," he said while pointing to each one of them. "Now listen...There is no self, so how can something that does not exist be liberated?" He began to laugh and laugh. "Can you imagine the absurdity?" he asked. "And the Absolute — this everything-ness — is not in bondage, is it? So how can it be liberated either? If you don't believe me, try to find the 'I' who you think you are. Go on, look for it, don't take my word for it, because I am nobody."

The old man laughed and then pushed his spiky finger into my chest. He said, "You want to be liberated, but think about what I just told you. Think about who it is who wants to be liberated. There's your problem, right there." He poked me again, leaving a bruise and a lingering soreness I could not dismiss.

The gardener waved his hand in dismissal at us, let out another little chuckle, and then ran his gnarled fingers through his short beard. He stared intently at me for a few seconds then picked up his walking stick and started off toward the ashram.

"Most who say they are seeking the Truth are full of ideas about what enlightenment should be and how to get it," Guru-ma told us. "They expect an explosion — a flash of brilliant insight, an out-of-body experience wrapped up in a thousand suns, the ability to see into the future or read minds, omnipresence, an aura that casts off rays of love in all directions, the ability to heal with their minds, or an all-encompassing rapture of warmth, love, and security. They expect eternal bliss and joy in a bolt from heaven. They think that they can be blasted away like a rocket liberating themselves from this earthly plane. Isn't it so? Maybe you are looking for godly music and the light of angelic beings paving the way to other realms. Or it could be that your idea of an enlightened being is one who sits in front of an audience of followers falling at his feet, or a sage from another century who can never be rivaled in his wisdom or purity because he is long gone. What game are you playing with all of this?"

The mind, Guru-ma said, is awash with concepts that try to define an indefinable reality. "One who sits on the outside, looking in at the one who is in full awareness is only seeing an image that he himself has created. Be your own being; stay your own course; live your own life. Uncover Truth without images and ideas directing you from the past or from second-hand information. An ancient misconception is nevertheless a misconception. Liberation is one of these misconceptions."

Guru-ma explained that preconceived ideas must be abandoned — surrendered — because the Truth is not an experience, it is a kind of knowing that does not involve the false identity of "I" and its grand collection of identities, desires to be better, memories, and judgments. Truth is sensed in complete and total quiet — stillness — because such a stateless state is that which is devoid of all form, movement, boundaries, action, and change. The self, on the other hand, is predicated upon change, busy-ness, ideas, comparisons, judgments, memories, and the persistent comings and goings of thoughts and forms, which is why it can never know the Truth that underlies it.

As the old man had said, the paradox is this: The self is a belief. Can a belief be liberated? Who or what is there to be liberated from a belief? A mirage cannot be bound and therefore cannot be set free. Does consciousness that exists prior to the self need to be liberated? No, because it is not bound by anything. Does the body need to be liberated? No, because the body alone has no sense of self-importance; it is a biological entity spending its every moment going through its myriad functions of survival. The self believes it is bound and in need of liberation, but if you stop identifying as this body and all that you think it has accrued and accomplished, then it becomes clear that making an effort to be liberated is chasing a dream.

The mind is so weighed down with the noise of fantasy, mystery, secrets, self-aggrandizement, self-centeredness, and feelings of specialness that it cannot see what is simply right here all the time. The essence of what you are, prior to the body and mind, is here, now. To know this requires dropping the belief that you are an individual who must be set free.

You are already what you seek.

Self-inquiry brings you to the gate of the Truth — the twelfth pillar

With one of her aides by her side, Guru-ma walked across the lawn, up the steps of the main building, and through the colonnade. As she walked, more and more people gathered behind her, slowly forming a long chain of devotees. I watched this happening as I sat alone beneath a tree across the way. As the scene unfolded, the crowd increased in size so that throngs were trying to squeeze through the doorway just to stay apace.

I got up from my resting place and walked across the lawn and into the main building where everyone was now getting settled. Guru-ma was helped into a seated position, and there she sat, legs crossed and back straight, in front of a big audience, waiting for everyone to quiet down. I stood by the door and leaned against the jamb. Suddenly, as if transformed into a spry young girl, Guru-ma leapt to her feet and shouted out, "Stop following me!" Then she quickly headed for the door, brushed past me, and continued along at a brisk pace until she disappeared through the gates of the ashram.

I turned to look at the stunned faces of the devotees now staring at the spot where Guru-ma had been only moments before. Some of them whispered to their neighbors with grave concern. Others were crying. Some had the expressions of mourners. Still others were looking around with a broad smile on their faces, as if they had just witnessed a big joke.

I walked away from the building and the audience full of puzzled inhabitants, and into the sunshine so that I could be alone to ponder Guru-ma's words. Moments later, I, too, walked through the gates of the ashram and onto the foothills nearby. All the while, Guru-ma's three little words were turning over and over in my mind.

Twenty minutes later I sat down beneath a shady tree and stared out at the lake in the distance. The sun was reflecting off the water, and the only sound available to me was the voice of Guru-ma calling out the words, "Stop following me!" so that they echoed off the walls of my mind.

I considered that Guru-ma had delivered her shocking, three-word speech as an invitation, not a rejection. She was inviting each person into their own selves, unencumbered by the words of the guru. One cannot realize one's true nature as a follower, as an accepter of the words or directions of any authority, even those of the guru.

For those who truly need to realize the Truth of who they are, there can be no authority to dictate the way. The door must opened by some other means.

How do you realize the Truth as your nature? Is there a method, a trick, or a system? What does it take to push away the false and to know the true? Yes, the guru can be instrumental in your search, but not when she is idolized as a revered object.

The same questions of "how" have been posed for thousands of years, and they imply that there is a method, means or path to the Truth. To think so is deceptive, because it suggests that there is a distance between you and what you truly are. How could there be?

There is no space or time to cover in order to realize your true nature, and yet, paradoxically, it seems to take time, or ripening. To the "I"-self, which separates itself from all other expressions, it seems to take work and effort to bring you from here to there. It seems to take direction, advice, and methods shrouded in secrets.

By mere definition, the Absolute is always present. It is you. It is here. It never leaves. It does not come and it does not go. It is the ever-present space in which every expression and thought dwells. There is literally no "getting to" it or attaining it as a state of being. All that needs to be done is to realize that the self is just a belief, an illusion, a mirage. And then what? It is a misconception that all thinking then comes to an end when this becomes known. Does the realization that a mirage is not actually a pool of water change the fact that it can still be seen after it is discovered not to be as it appears? The mirage remains, yet the belief that it is water does not.

Having fragmented the wholeness of existence into the sense of me-versus-you, subject and object, the self is concerned with questions of who, where, what, how, why, and when. But none of these questions apply to the Absolute, because the Absolute is not an object. Once you realize you are the subject as well the perceived object, then you have realized the Truth. Without objects, without fragmentation, there is only oneness, a unity, a wholeness to reality.

Guru-ma had said, "Inquire into your self and you will find that there is nowhere to go and nothing new to be found."

And I thought deeply about her admonition to stop following her. She was saying that, if what you have realized is not due to your own observation of reality, then you are just living your life according to the information that comes from others, even the guru herself. If you really inquire into this, you will find that there is very little that you know that is not attached in some way to an idea that has been forwarded to you by other people, whether from your parents, or down through the ages of human history. What you know comes from the past; what is the point in living in the past? The past is static, stifling, and unyielding. You, without the belief of an "I," are only the present, not the past or future.

The self, based on nothing more than psychological conditioning, is adept at making assumptions and believing these assumptions are truths. Billions of people are convinced that there is a god that directs and intercedes in their lives, but this notion is not from their own experience. Even if one were to have a fantastic, "religious" experience, the very attributing of it to a god, karma, or purposeful intent is no more than an idea. Ask yourself what it is that you presume without really knowing through your own observation. Guru-ma told me that "it takes self-honesty to do this; surrender your pretenses, your past, and your identities. Why do you find it necessary to interpret your experiences, defend them as real, share them with others with great conviction, or infuse them with ideas that have been passed along to you? Find out for yourself how the I-thought makes conclusions and harbors beliefs based upon its own self-interests. If you want to know about God, then do not seek God; instead, seek who it is who wants to know."

Disregard everything you have heard pertaining to what you should find, experience, or become in the process of self-inquiry. Drop the ideas and expectations. Be your own pioneer into your deepest sense of being. Here, the guru is invaluable. A true self-realized teacher will be able to guide you inward without biasing you with statements that will keep you striving for some outward goal or expectation for an experience. But know this: The words of the guru are important only because of what they are pointing to.

On more than one occasion, Guru-ma had told me, "Realization of your true nature comes about by taking an earnest and total look at the self. This is a process of self-inquiry. No one but you can do this for yourself. This is how you come upon first-hand knowledge. No amount of information, philosophy, wisdom of a guru, or sage advice can replace your own observation. After all, who else but you can tell you what it is like to exist? Can your own mother tell you what you are feeling and see the thoughts that keep you awake at night? Who else but you knows how you think, what has affected you, where your ideas come from, and how it feels to know you live. You also may come to know what it is like to be free of the constructed sense of self."

Months passed since Guru-ma had told her flock to stop following her. Insulted and disheartened, many dropped out and found new gurus for themselves. Others supposed she had been testing them, and they clung ever tighter to her words, trying to find the mystery that must have underscored them. And there were a very few who began to listen to what she said and to use her words to observe their own minds.

Near the end of the rainy season, as happened every year, a new wave of visitors came to find Guru-ma. On one particular day a well-to-do, middle-aged doctor with plenty of worldly experience came to sit before her.

"What can you tell us that we can take away from this place and hold onto?" asked the doctor. "Naturally, I must return to my world, to my patients, and to the stress I face every day at home and at work."

"I cannot be your observation, inquiring into the depths of you. Nor can I think for you. This you must do for yourself," Guru-ma told him.

The doctor sat uncomfortably, trying to cross his legs on the hard floor, but he could not do so because he was obviously inflexible. The sight of him wriggling to find a suitable position led Guru-ma to invite him to sit any way he felt most comfortable. She offered him a chair, but he refused and decided to put his legs out in front of him and lean back on his outstretched hands.

"I thought that thinking was wrong," the doctor said. "Isn't the mind the whole problem?"

Guru-ma answered, "You are a clever man. This is a good question."

"Thank you," he proudly said while winking at the lady beside him.

"The tool that you call thinking has been used to discover and invent the world around you. Is it not so?" said Guru-ma. "Thinking is most practical and valuable. But at some point the mind turns inward to have a look at the sense of self. This is not to say that you think yourself into realization by a logical process. Rather, you use the mind to inquire deep within the psyche, and to closely observe the true nature of emotions, thoughts, relationships, ideas, memories, identities, possessions, and what lies behind all of this. Do not overlook this last point — to find what lies behind it all, because this is when the mind is most useful, as a tool of inquiry that brings all into conscious awareness. Ask yourself questions, challenge yourself. But do not search for answers; let them come. This has to be done without judgments, preconceived notions, jumping to conclusions, the making of images, or even adopting the language of spirituality. It means to merely observe the self so that you can get to the bottom of it, become aware of its nature, and ultimately find out whether it exists at all. And then, beyond this egoic mind, find out what is deeper and more subtle. Keep going until you find the vastness that is permanent and prior to all movement and form. This is where you will uncover what you are as the not-self."

This statement overwhelmed Guru-ma's audience, leaving in its wake a room full of confused, dazed, and even bored expressions. She waited a little while before continuing.

"Who knows how you eventually come to realize your true nature? Something sets off a spark and then everything changes. What is the catalyst — a book, going to lectures, sitting at a guru's feet, worshipping images or people, moving into yoga postures, directing your Kundalini energy, receiving a special transmission or gaze from a guru, or sitting silently in meditation as you focus on your breath? Maybe you will be struck by lightning."

The doctor laughed and said, "If you are hit by a bolt of lightning, I'm afraid there is little I can do for you."

Guru-ma smiled.

The doctor said, "I had heard that the guru can transmit enlightenment by being in one's presence. I have to admit, this is why I have come all this way to see you."

"Do you think it matters to me whether you come here to visit?" Guru-ma said. She rubbed her arm with her open palm, then held her hand up for everyone to see. She said, "Look. Nothing rubs off. Nothing rubs off of me and onto you when you sit beside me or touch my feet. You do this for you, not for me, and sitting near me has nothing to do with you turning the mind inward to find your true nature, does it?"

"But," said the doctor, "it's true that being in the presence of the guru has a profound effect on people, no?..."

Guru-ma interrupted him, saying, "It may indeed, but be careful not to make the guru into an object. Do you see? Being in the presence of a guru may be quite helpful for some. Quite helpful. A guru who has found her true nature can point you in the right direction, and this may be invaluable. But this is not about giving answers or transmitting energy. It is about pointing. You yourself must travel the road alone. It is your road, not mine, and not anyone else's. Sitting with the guru is not a replacement for the process of self-inquiry. That must be done nevertheless. If one is meant to know the Truth, being in the company of the guru can help immensely. But if one is meant to find one's true nature, and there is no guru — including books, videos, and so on — it can still be done, but it will be much harder, if next to impossible. When one is ready, the guru appears. This can be in many different forms. It is not a mystical occurrence, but rather one wherein consciousness makes it so," said Guru-ma.

"Worshipping the guru as an object will achieve very little," said the doctor, trying to absorb what he was being taught.

"Yes," Guru-ma continued. "This is a practice that the self likes to embrace. It may want to be a follower and a devotee, maybe even thinking that its own station is elevated by means of association with one greater and more powerful. But we are all of the same cloth, without status or separation. So what is it that you really want? A teacher for the sake of having a teacher, or to allow the teacher's words to lead you inward?"

Guru-ma turned her attention to the rest of her audience and said, "Very few people have any interest in pursuing that which lies behind all existence and who they are behind this facade of the self. But those who do must consider the question: "What is it that I want?" If you want peace and calmness, entertainment, a sense of belonging, someone to fawn over, to experience a special feeling, to become a spiritual teacher, to see a bright light, to hear heavenly music, to build your powers of imagination, or to have a way to feel good about yourself, then do what you want to bring these into your life. There is nothing wrong with any such thing. Just know that none of these have anything to do with realizing the fundamental Truth or a direct way to uncover it."

There was an invaluable lesson that came from Guru-ma that day. I was moved once again to earnestly turn my mind to the practice of self-inquiry and how it might work for me. I thought I had been doing this all along, but something had been missing. Of course, I had already spent countless hours inquiring into my own nature, but now there was something more going on. I could not put my finger on it, but there was a ghost of a concept somewhere in my psyche.

Guru-ma had always reduced her teachings into one simple message, regardless of the question anyone had to pose. She would always say that one should ponder the question "Who am I?" But now this question took on a new shade for me, and I felt there was something deep beyond, beneath, or perhaps behind the mind and all existence that I was not seeing. What could this be, and what did it mean to uncover it?

Guru-ma had said that a self-realized guru can inspire you to realize your true nature if you take her words to heart. "However," she said, "you should be clear about what it is you want. You have to be honest with yourself. Do you want entertainment? To be a follower or a leader? To study? To have spiritual experiences? To talk about fascinating aspects of spirituality with your friends? Do you want to create your own following of devotees? There are millions who give over their hearts and minds to spiritual and religious leaders. The world is rife with such teachers and followers; however, only a few of these teachers have realized their true nature. Many manipulate their devotees in their self-styled cults, while others may be well-intentioned yet as self-deluded and neurotic as their followers. What is it that *you* want?"

A true guru will show you the way to yourself by leading you to delve into that which you call "I."

Self-inquiry is not a practice or method; it is attention on the self. Through observation you fully come to realize the very nature of the self, thoughts, consciousness, and life. Self-inquiry will not be embraced by most people, because it takes persistent attention, unyielding interest, and courage to face and question the validity of the "I." The self is resistant and afraid to change, because it fears obsolescence, diminishment, and death. There has to be such a burning desire to get to the bottom of it all that nothing else takes precedence.

In the course of looking at the self and the contents of consciousness, at times it seemed that I was on a journey along a lonely road in the depths of the night, but I knew that the fear of the darkness had to be embraced. I had to come to know the ultimate reality by first seeing if there was a reality to the "I." I kept Guru-ma's teaching in mind when she said, "At some point, you must abandon even the desire and effort so that you can just 'be.' This is the essence of surrender."

My friend whom I had met on the train so long ago had explained this balance as the razor's edge: Where and when does the effort stop so that the "being" can simply be?

She had told me, "Inquire. Find out if the body knows anything at all. Does it say that it, or others, are beautiful or ugly? Does the body alone claim that someone has stolen your possessions or told you something hurtful? Does it criticize others or crave religious teachings? No. The body, a biological entity, just exists, moves, procreates, sleeps, functions, eats, seeks shelter, and so on. What does the self need in order to be convinced that it is not this body? It needs only to step aside so that the Truth may be evident. This is something that you may only observe for yourself. Otherwise, it remains a second-hand teaching for you to accept or deny.

"It is only the false self, the ego mind, that gets dejected, confused, and frustrated while searching for this Truth. It is this sense of self that states, 'I am almost there,' or 'I don't quite get it yet,' and 'I am still trying.' When this happens, again and again, you must go deeply into the question, 'Who am I?' The true guru will remind you of this and direct you back to the self-inquiry process."

The answer to despair is despair — the thirteenth pillar

On the last day of her visit, I met my friend in the gardens after breakfast so that I could try to get to the bottom of this egoic mind. As always, her face was glowing with an otherworldliness, and her eyes sparkled with life. I, on the other hand, was lost. My head was swimming with information about spiritual truths, but my world remained disconnected, fragmented, and ill-at-ease. I had answers, but they were not answers. I held facts, conclusions, and concepts, but these were things I had picked up from hearing so many talks and listening to so many words.

We sat down beside a small pond, and she warmly took hold of my hand. Her gaze seemed to melt me, and I allowed her familiar motherly compassion to wash over me.

"You look so sad," she said.

"What I have learned," I said. "is worth nothing at all without the realization of who I am. What good is so much knowledge about the way things are? It's like being able to describe all the properties of a mountain without ever having set foot on one."

She shook her head in agreement and squeezed my hand.

"Quite so," she said.

Her long, golden earrings caught the sunlight and flashed at me. I told her that, day in and day out, in silence and solitude, I had meditated on the nature of my true beingness, as existence. For the longest time I had tried to see the world as one totality, and to perceive others as the same as me. I tried shutting out my mind and turning it off. I worked to understand the cosmology of the mind, body, consciousness, and silence. I learned that language can only be a pointer, and that words could not describe what the mind has no capacity to realize. Still, I tortured myself with questions I could not answer, and I had suffered from my inability to be free from this apparent bondage of the mind. All I had were words, and they clung to the inside of my brain as if they had any real value.

"And now?" she asked.

"And now I don't know what to do. I feel like giving up. What can I do?" I begged of her. "I have not learned a thing, and perhaps my time has been wasted on gathering information. I am still suffering, and there is no effort that I can expend to lead me any closer to the Truth. In fact," I continued, "I have done everything that Guru-ma has led me to do in looking deeply inward. I have rejected all authority so that my ideas are my own..."

When I had nothing more to say, my friend kindly offered these words spoken slowly and clearly: "You must know this 'I' whom you insist is suffering. Who is it who separates the self from the whole? You have rejected authorities, so you have said. But what about the authority of you, yourself? What are you holding onto in there? Look at this from the other way around."

She stood up, and then before she left me she said, "The answer to despair is despair. No more words."

I watched her walk away, and her multi-colored dress lit up the path that she ascended on her way to Guru-ma's apartment.

Had my friend left me with yet one more riddle? Maybe there were two more riddles: The answer to despair is despair, and that there was something called "the authority of me."

I was numb by what she had told me. I had not even figured out what it meant to know who I was, and now this! My immediate inclination was to lash out in anger, but I could do no such thing, and the anger never materialized.

I sat thinking of my friend and the peace that she exuded. It made me trust her even more than Guru-ma. Each time we had met, I found myself in her reflection. What was I thinking? Why was there a need for such comparisons? Comparisons create conflict, and that's the last thing that I wanted. I let the foolish ideas go, realizing that it was this self that was causing a distraction, so I put my attention back on what my friend had said to me. She was pointing me to something, and, despite my mental state, I resolved to find out what.

Though my mind was inclined to place blame on someone for my despair, it could not begin to muster the strength to find a scapegoat. The slightest of urges begged me to run after my friend before she disappeared into the building across the courtyard so that I could confront her. But in observing this impulse as not belonging to me, half-heartedly acting as a relic from the past, without interest or action, it dissipated as fast as it had appeared. All I could do was mull over the latest in a series of enigmatic words.

I decided I had to be alone, without the distraction of others, so I wandered far away from the ashram and retreated into the mountains as I had done so often to escape the presence of humanity. I hiked for quite some time until I was high enough to view the world down below — the foothills, quiet lake, scattered buildings, lush jungle, and the guru's tiny hut with its gleaming white roof. I sat for hours and hours, and the day passed in meditation. I ignored all urges to eat or sleep, and I just sat like a stone among millions of others. When the sun went down, the intense blackness of night happily overtook me. The stars came out in full force beneath a rare, cloudless sky, and a slight breeze kept the insects at bay. The immensity of the scene before me tugged at my sense of awe of this universe, and at last I began to relax this weary mind and body. I removed my shirt, rolled it into a pillow, and then laid down to stare at the sparkling heavens.

I mouthed the words of my kind friend as if they were a mantra — "the answer to despair is despair."

Lying in the dark and melding into the night, eventually I realized that this was no riddle at all. It slowly occurred to me that it always had turned out that whatever emotion I had exhibited was inseparable from me as the self. Who was I? — I was the one who was stuck in this egoic mind. The very word "I" had throughout my life represented the conditioned self. Although this was a conclusion I had reached long ago, now this notion somehow had become illuminating and no longer just an abstract bit of information that my sense of individuality proudly embraced. It was a knowingness, devoid of emotion, and independent of ownership. When I had been angry, I realized that I had been anger itself. When I had been greedy, then it turned out that I had been greed. When I had meditated, I was also that which was meditated upon. My anger had always led to my finding anger in others. It was as if I had a lifetime full of unifying my mental tendencies with the people and situations that enabled me to live out every emotion embedded within this being whom I called "I." And now I was facing despair. What could this be telling me?

What was the resolution for any of this madness? How could I be such a ball of terrible emotions without the chance of escaping from them? It was apparent as well, that the whole world is, and always has been, full of people suffering in the same way, but to varying degrees. They suffer from ignorance of their own nature, continually making life difficult for themselves, and meeting the same hardships over and over to fulfill the demands of their strong thoughts that are called emotions.

I seemed to have stumbled onto the reason for endless suffering throughout the ages — that it is rooted deeply in the ignorance of who we are as perceived individuals mired in conditioned emotions and thoughts that express themselves in our interactions, relationships, and experiences. We *become* the situations and thoughts that lie in wait in an unformed cloud of potentiality called consciousness. In other words, anger finds anger as an object, and it knows this object because the subject and object are contained in the same oneness. The self knows only conflict because it is not realizing that it is all that it sees and experiences. The observer is the observed. How simple!

One's anger leads one to focus on the angry people, thoughts, and situations that are already existent in consciousness in which all is contained. Rather than knowing that it is the whole, the self believes there are only fragments, and it experiences the fragments that it is most conditioned to be drawn to. This is the way every emotion and mental tendency creates our reality, and the world is full of people doing this same crazy thing without cessation. No wonder, I thought, there is so much suffering; how could there not be? Everyone is in a state of self-made, perpetual conflict!

Now I was inquiring into the matter of despair. Not only despair as a concept, but despair as this self, this "I." It did not take me long to see that I was despair itself. I was despair, and therefore despair was my reality. What did this mean?

I sat up and stared at the moonlight reflecting off the lake. Neither the moon nor the water were the source of light, but only a reflection. The "I" is the moon, and the Truth is the sun.

I took my inquiry with me back to my room. I slept deeply that night with a clear mind, thinking no more of this matter of myself as despair until I woke up in the morning. And several days later, while I had given up thinking about it altogether, something transformative occurred. On that day, I was simply walking down a familiar, well-worn dirt path, daydreaming about my childhood, when I stopped to stare up at two monkeys noisily playing on the tree branches. That's when it occurred to me that despair is the act of giving up. This is how I had defined it. So, the answer had to be that I had to give up. Then I thought about this idea of an inner authority that my friend had mentioned.

While I had rooted out all the ideas and values of authority that I had collected throughout my years from teachers, writers, priests, school books, parents, and so on, I had not taken a careful look at this concept of an inner authority. I had created my own divisive, distracting, and limiting beliefs and made them real and valuable. They were self-created and held with great conviction, and I had to give them up.

Though I had asked myself "Who am I?" over and over again, I now came to consider not only the obvious teachings and impact of those who had influenced me, but as importantly, my own mind that had experiences that led to opinions, fears, and paradigms. These self-made ideas were a strong component of the self. I knew I must drop them —

surrender them to the inner guru, the one who is me at the core.

And so I I meditated — not by sitting in a lotus position and concentrating on my breath or anything else of the sort, but rather by thinking, inquiring into this inner self-made authority. I soon discovered that my mind had been brimming with so many self-induced opinions and values. I was my own authority, and this authority had been compounded by other authorities along the way. And this led me back to the idea that the answer to despair must be despair itself. It now made sense. I had to give up on everything — especially my self.

Perhaps you will one day hear someone say, as I had, that the answer to despair is despair. Or maybe it will be phrased in some other way. In any case, the message will be the same. In my life I had despaired over all my problems. Then, when seeking the Truth of reality itself, I despaired over not being able to awaken to this true nature of which the gurus had talked about so often that all meaning had leached completely out of the words.

What are these self-imposed opinions and concepts that we grasp onto as if words had any value? We hear that being awake — experiencing the ultimate enlightenment — is blissful and all our worldly troubles evaporate like a puddle in the summer heat. We remember someone having said that all thoughts shall vanish from the brain, and we shall walk around with an empty head free of any ideas to bother us. I asked myself, where is the Truth in any of this information? What did I know for myself? Almost nothing.

I considered the multitude of concepts not of my own discovery. I realized they must be brushed aside to keep them from distracting me from knowing what would otherwise be painfully obvious.

I thought about how many times I had cried out that I was confused and just couldn't "get it," but I did not take a step back and realize that the only confusion lies with the staunchness of the self. There is no "I" to "get" or become anything. The Truth is always present. The absolute, undivided totality sits quietly behind all movement and form, ever-present. All that is permanent and essential is Now, and this Truth that is at the core cannot become anything, because it is prime. There is no arriving, becoming, receiving or getting; there is only seeing what already is.

Perhaps you suffer, as I had, over the inability to find that one secret — the key to making the realization of your true nature become apparent to you. You seek the "how," but cannot find it. You want to end suffering yet you perpetuate the self. You cannot quell the mind, so you try harder and harder to become something that you have as a goal in the form of an image that you or someone else has made. Eventually the mind and body become defeated so that you meet with despair, having come to the end of your rope, exhausted from the futility of it all. All of your searching, thinking, learning, and introspection has worn you out. What will you do when you are standing at this threshold?

The solution to your despair is despair itself. This idea, seeming at first to be a magnificent koan or an outrageous paradox, set me off to look into the meaning of despair. I deconstructed its importance and context until at last I saw that it implies giving up. When this dawned on me, I at once realized that the mind – this yearning, struggling self — must give up. It must let go of both the outer and inner authority that comprises all mental tendencies. Then I recalled another piece of sage advice: "Surrender to the guru."

Surrender. Is this not related to despair for someone who has nothing else to give or lose? When you hear that you must surrender, do not jump into this without due diligence. You have to be ever so careful, because if you take this the wrong way, then you will remain in the continuous loop of a world created and perpetuated by the self. Tread lightly, for you are on the verge of knowing. You have come to the razor's edge.

As with most other axioms, take care not to misinterpret the meaning of "surrender to the guru" according to the self's limited attempts at rationalization. You are doing nothing more than giving up a belief; and the guru is you.

Taking my friend's loving advice deep into my heart, I meditated long and hard about the notion of despair and its implications of surrender. Then I stepped back and observed the process of my own transformation. At first I had denied that her words were befitting of my situation. My mind wanted to dismiss them. Next, I grew angry, as the self fought to defend and protect itself from annihilation. Then I grew heavy with concern over whether my giving up all effort would result in the abandonment of any hope for realization of my own nature as the Absolute. Next, I needed to drop any ideas of the Absolute, the self, consciousness, and all else; they were not mine, but rather concepts I had accepted from others. More information, more distractions.

I pleaded to unknown forces within myself for salvation. I knew that effort itself was my final obstacle, and that my friend was right. Giving up was the only thing I had not yet tried — giving up effort in favor of simply being.

Giving up.

I had to give up trying to figure everything out as if it were a puzzle that only hard work and time could solve. I had to stop searching and hoping to become something. I had to give up trying and searching immediately. I had to give up the need to know. I had to give up expectations, concepts, ideas, and memories of what I should be and what I was not. I had to give up my preconceived notions of what a guru should be or how I might become one. I had to give up the inner authorities I had created with all my values and stubborn opinions. I had to give up all language, descriptions, and images. I had to stop hanging onto words and dissecting them for deeper meanings. I had to retreat into this inner being who had always, throughout my life, observed everything in silence while all manner of action and relationships took place in this frenetic, confusing world.

In stillness alone was the answer; I had to completely surrender the idea that I was an individual.

But there was even more to this. I had to stop cursing the mind and trying to fashion it into something that could be enlightened, improved, or tamed. I was soon to discover that it had been my point-of-view all along, as an individual self and body, that had been creating and perpetuating all my suffering and searching. And nearly everyone else is also stuck in this same pattern, living each moment in ignorance, darkness, expectation, delusion, elation, memories, frustration, hope, despair, and suffering — living each moment only as it relates to the past and is projected into the future to create a never-ending stream of fear and separation from the unity of all things. In this typical, ubiquitous cycle, at best there existed the pleasant, and at worse came the pain.

Standing alone on a rugged mountain path, in the heart of a misty, lush landscape, overlooking the ashram and a stream of well-meaning pilgrims down below, I became overwhelmed by a feeling of endless, bottomless sorrow. The people milling about were lost, as was I, ever-searching to be whole again. Some knew this instinctively, while others did not. We were all searching for something that was neither hidden nor apart from ourselves.

As the feeling of sorrow bled out to the edges of my skin, I could not hold the burden of this suffering, and I fell to my knees. This was not the typical sorrow of self-pity; it was something else, much bigger and less personal. And it continued to expand, beyond the borders of this insignificant body, and I began to sob, as wave after wave of sorrow overtook me. This was not merely my own sorrow, but rather the suffering of all humankind — a shared suffering that ignorance of the true Heart had caused. The sorrow was love in some strange way that words fail to describe. It was a river, deep and wide, without any personal sense to it.

As if to mirror what was going on inside of me, the sky quickly grew gray with thick clouds, and the sun disappeared behind them, cooling the air that swirled around me. Leaves and blades of grass found no stillness, and they rustled and clicked loudly across the landscape. Birds took flight from the branches, and a colorful snake slithered past me to find shelter beneath a rock. And this heavy, heavy sorrow only grew stronger.

This tremendous oppression by which I was now fully consumed was so great that my chest ached and I clutched it with both hands, wondering if I were about to die of a broken heart. A bolt of lightning lit up the sky and landscape, followed by a deafening clap of thunder that rocked and vibrated the earth. I laid down and curled up on the ground, weeping uncontrollably with my face pressed into coarse gravel and ancient dirt. And then it began to rain.

Seconds later, the water was pouring down in great sheets from the sky, soaking me to the skin. And it pounded the ground around and beside me, and onto the vast the landscape so that nothing was spared. I came to sense every space and cell of this body, because I was this body. I was this mind and self, and yet I was not mind nor body nor anything at all. But, at the same instant, I was all. And this "I" could no longer be not contained; it was itself the container. So deafening was the torrential rain that nothing else could be heard or seen — no thoughts, body, surroundings, or even the suffering of this expression nor of humanity.

Unable to find the ground so I could lift up this listless body, I laid still in the din, melding with the earth. Every kernel of life was relentlessly pounded by the rain so that nothing could escape the cleansing. And the water ran swiftly into streams and tributaries, down the mountainsides, into the lake, washing over hills, and pooling in valleys. Vibrating and aware, the trees, flowers, rocks, blades of grass, weeds, and shrubs were silent sentinels to witness my fingers clinging to the soil, and my eyes opening to see the edges of my beingness dissolve into the wholeness. The shower was coming down so forcefully that there was nothing but a wall of water blinding me to the world, and the sound was so immense that even thoughts could not be noticed.

I strained to see if I was caught up in some mystical vortex or held in the arms of God, but there was no such poetry or mysticism to be known. There was no experience, no sightings of otherworldly beings, and no wondrous insights into the great beyond. No. There was nothing but life, existence in full measure. I was now what I always had been — insignificant and indistinguishable from all there was. In my head I heard my friend and Guru-ma in unison say, "I am nothing," and now, too, I was nothing. And yet I was everything — bodiless, formless, expressionless, without beginning or end. At that instant, I realized that I, as the small self, as if turned off by a switch, stopped fragmenting the whole of existence as I melded with the world. There was no longer an inner and outer, an up or down, a great or small.

And until this very moment, throughout my life, I had all along been looking at the wholeness, yet believing that this wholeness was a collection of pieces. I had for so long embodied ignorance — living in perpetual ignorance of the wholeness only because the self had been fixating and focusing on the mental tendencies it had created from a lifetime of conditioning. Now here I was, lying on the ground, washing away, and I had not become anything new or different; nothing mystical had taken place, nothing startling or explosive. Lying still in the quiet of the calamitous din, I had simply realized what I had been all along. And now the river of sorrow flowed ever so strong and steadily, but no longer for the "I" that ceased to be.

Besides knowing that "I am," there was nothing else to know or be; there was nothing more and nothing less. And even the "I am" would yield to all and to nothingness.

The 'I' has changed its meaning

At the gate of the ashram, Guru-ma took both of my hands in hers and said, "There's nothing left for you here. Abide in who you are." She smiled, pressed her forehead against mine, and then I entered the continuous flow of people descending the mountain and onto the busy, dusty road leading back to the railway station.

The long trek back to the village of my birth took nearly two months. Along the way I stopped to see my friend, the lady who had led me to find Guru-ma. We spent two days together, and on the first evening of my visit I asked her, "Now what happens?"

"Look what has already appeared to happen," she said. "You have realized what most people fear the most — this entity we each learn to call 'I' is not to be found at all. You have always been pure consciousness yet never realized it because you were lost in a belief. Life will continue on, and the body will age. Events, people, animals, objects, and nature all appear in consciousness. They shall continue to rise and fall, and you now know them to be temporal expressions. To others you will look like any other person with his idiosyncrasies and personality traits, but you will look at them and see the struggles and suffering that were once yours. In this awareness there will be compassion, because in them you see yourself as I sit here knowing myself as you."

On our last morning together, just before sunrise, my guru fed me breakfast, gave me enough provisions to last for the next several days, and then wished me a peaceful journey home. Setting off in a heavy mist that had enveloped the world in a wondrous and refreshing fog, I was once again on my way home.

I cannot begin to explain the specific details of how this complete surrender of the mind, body, and all conditioning had led to the realization of my true nature, because then you may perhaps make a study out of me, and that will not help you at all. I offer you no methodology, instruction, or process. I only offer you pointers — *Pillars*, if you will — because this is all that is possible to do.

If you desperately want to know your true nature by transcending the self, then pay attention to the "I am." Ask yourself who you are, and then look for the answer with all of the attention, courage, and honesty you can muster. Dig deep until you find the substratum of all that is. This is where you will discover yourself. And, in so doing, you will find that there is only an absoluteness where there once seemed only to be an "I" and a world of objects. You will realize that you are that which you had been seeking.

This "I" that I now call myself for the sake of convenience has changed its meaning. It is no longer the same "I" that was once claimed by, and as, the self. It is something altogether different, and there is no name for it. This essential "I" remains ever silent, ever still, ever aware, and never changing, regardless of the actions of people, the progression of life, aging, words and language, violence or peace, the arising and dissolution of forms, the rise and fall of emotions, the appearance of thoughts, and even death and birth. Everything continues to happen in the world, but nothing happens to this "I."

To the mind that is not ready to listen, my final words shall seem impossible to understand: The ultimate Truth exists in silence, behind all existence, and at the same time, permeating it. And this is who you are.

Epilogue:
Returning home

I returned to my village after the rainy season to discover that my mother had passed away less than a year prior to my arrival. Brokenhearted by her death, my father fell ill, retired from his business, and went to live with my brother and his family in a distant village where my sister-in-law's family had lived for centuries.

Just before dawn one morning I took a long stroll along the beach that I had known throughout my youth. I mused over how, like the sun, life appears to be but a flame. As such, this body is lit at birth, burns brightly with the vigor of youth, and is extinguished at the end of its fateful journey. In between all milestones, the body, imbued with consciousness, has a brief and shining opportunity in which to know its true nature. For nearly all, the mind sinks deeply into a dreamy play of its own making, and it cannot see its way out of this creation so that a continuous cycle of pain and pleasure is the only experience to be had.

As I stood with my feet buried in the sand, and with the world beginning to stir, I watched as a sole seagull landed at the surf's edge. Off in the distance, a handful of fishermen cast their nets into the ocean and reminded me of my father. I took in a deep breath of misty, salty air and closed my eyes for a moment. Then I smiled and turned my face to the rising sun.

I made my way to a once-familiar coconut tree that had seen a hundred seasons come and go. Beneath it I spread out a small blanket and sat with my back against the rough trunk to soak in the silent stillness, remaining absent of intent or focus on anything in particular, neither inside of the body nor outside of it. No time had passed since I had sat in this same spot, as a boy who suffered so deeply that nothing could slake his thirst for the ultimate Truth. And these are the words that came to mind:

You may run down a list of ten thousand things that make up part of what is called reality — thoughts, ideas, the body, the senses, the elements of the earth, experiences, forms — and then eliminate them one by one, or all at once, so that there is nothing left. What then remains?

Eliminate the ability to describe, use a name, speak, form images, and communicate. What then remains? Next, remove everything physical and nonphysical, and everything spiritual, religious, historical, philosophical, and scientific. What then remains? Rule out the elements that comprise all that you see, touch, hear, taste, and smell. Set aside the body, the mind, all thought forms, all expressions, all creatures, and nature. What then remains? Next, set aside all that is inherent to the body and earth — air, water, energy, warmth, dampness, heat, cold, coolness, and so on. What then remains? Do away with light, sound, depth, breadth, width, space, and time, and what yet remains? Disregard all that changes, grows, lives, dies, ages, becomes more beautiful or ugly, as well as all duality that includes pairs of opposites, and what remains? Find for yourself what remains when all you can know has been eliminated, and this is what you are.

And, as a seed contains the life to be expressed, in this nothingness is the everythingness of the mind, spirit, body, and potentiality of consciousness.

Existence exists. Beneath it is an infinite nothingness that contains everything. See if this is both inner and outer, or neither. See if it is you, the ultimate Self. Can this Absolute be explained, put into words, or conveyed to another? Is it an experience, an object? Must one search for the existence that they already are?

While the warm, sentient, breathing, living person may say, "I am," or "I exist," existence itself continues regardless of the death of that person, the birth of another, or the appearance or disappearance of all persons, nature, objects, and even knowledge. Like the space that contains all that exists, behind this lies the Absolute Truth, independent of what goes on inside of it, prior to action and the expression into form, as well as thought and consciousness. It is the container, the contained, and the containing. And yet it is not a container nor anything at all. The mind can never know it, yet it can be sensed. But these are words attempting to describe the indescribable. Even the words must be surrendered.

I closed my eyes and soaked in the rhythm of the ocean as it welcomed this body home. Here I was in the same place, with my toes buried in the same warm sand, listening to the same waves under the same sky. Yet nothing and all was the same. The body had changed, but the presence — behind and throughout existence itself — had remained, as it always does, unchanged, immeasurable, unbounded, and indescribable.

Life had been a dream from the moment I had first declared, "I am."

Only words

Although words can never convey what is unexplainable, there are certain terms that appear in this book that would be helpful to know:

Absolute: The Absolute is a term used to point to that which contains all; the oneness, the unity, and the silent stillness that lies beyond and behind all movement, including consciousness. It is prime, and therefore indescribable, immeasurable, boundless, invisible, stateless, and infinite.

Consciousness: Consciousness is a word that few people, even "experts" are able to define and agree upon. It is that from which springs all forms, expression, movement, action, thought, and that which we call life. Consciousness is both the latent and the manifest. It is a field of possibilities. It is also awareness. It is the orchestrator, the orchestrated, and the orchestrating. It is the seer and the seen, the meditator and the meditated.

Enlightenment: While the word enlightenment may be used to describe the state of a person who has realized his/her true self as not-the-mind and not-the-body, it points to a paradox. This is because the self (that which is called "I") is an accretion of thoughts and therefore just a belief; and a belief cannot be enlightened. And the Absolute, which is the true reality that incorporates all, cannot be enlightened because it is prior to all action and is already whole.

Guru: A guru is any source from which you may learn. It may be a friend, a teacher, a sage, a book, a monk, or even an enemy. Traditionally, a guru is a person who leads you to discover reality for yourself.

Meditation: There are many types of meditation taught by spiritual traditions. But the meditation that leads to the realization of one's true nature is not a passive method.

Meditation of this type, called *self-inquiry*, has to do with the intense observation of all aspects of the I-self and its source. It is not focus, and it is not centered upon the body, its breathing, or its vital signs. It is not intended to make one happier, more relaxed, a better person, or more aware. It has nothing to do with trying to quiet or control the mind.

Mind and self: The mind is a complex instrument, and in simpler terms it represents both the mind that is practical so that it remembers and can operate in reality, as well as the self. The self may also be called the psychological mind, ego, or the sense of "me" or "I." It is a construct formed by the accretion of thought. The self is created by conditioning of education, teachings, exposure to ideas, memories, input from the senses, judgments, assessments, and beliefs. The self is a belief that has sandwiched itself between the physical body and consciousness.

Self-inquiry: This is a method of introspection brought about by meditating on the "I," thoughts, consciousness, and the Absolute. The purpose of self-inquiry is to realize your own true nature.

Truth: While truth is often used to explain an individual's assessment of reality, in this book Truth refers to the ultimate reality — the Absolute — that is not subject to the interpretation, perspective, or creation of the mind.

Made in United States
Orlando, FL
12 January 2022